The ma

Dani's gaze followed his arms as he raised them. Then her heart all but stopped. He held an enormous wooden stake, and its point was aimed directly at her heart!

"Stop!" A deep male voice boomed across the room. "I will not allow this!"

"'Tis Karsten," someone whispered.

The second man swooped out of the darkness and swept Dani into his arms. Then he strode outside, hoisted her onto a black stallion and leapt up behind her, saying, "Let's go, Ebony."

The animal took off like the wind, and they raced along beneath the harvest moon. A hundred questions were begging for answers, but Dani couldn't ask them...not while she was hurtling through the night on a galloping horse, pressed against this dark, mysterious stranger.

Dear Reader,

What else can be more romantic *and* more mysterious than traveling through time to meet the man who was destined to share your life? We're especially proud to present TIMELESS LOVE, a unique new program in Harlequin Intrigue that will showcase these much-loved time-travel stories.

So journey back with Dawn Stewardson to Transylvania in 1850, where Dani Patton awakens—surrounded by villagers who believe she's a vampire! Could the man in the black cape who rescues her on his stallion really be the man of her dreams? Join us and find out!

We hope you enjoy *Hunter's Moon*...and all the special books coming to you in the months ahead in TIMELESS LOVE.

Sincerely,

Debra Matteucci
Senior Editor & Editorial Coodinator
Harlequin Books
300 East 42nd Street
New York, NY 10017

Hunter's Moon
Dawn Stewardson

Harlequin Books

TORONTO • NEW YORK • LONDON
AMSTERDAM • PARIS • SYDNEY • HAMBURG
STOCKHOLM • ATHENS • TOKYO • MILAN
MADRID • WARSAW • BUDAPEST • AUCKLAND

To my editor, Julianne Moore, who envisioned the book's opening.
To my parents, who helped play with the plot.
And to John, always.

ISBN 0-373-22281-5

HUNTER'S MOON

Copyright © 1994 by Dawn Stewardson

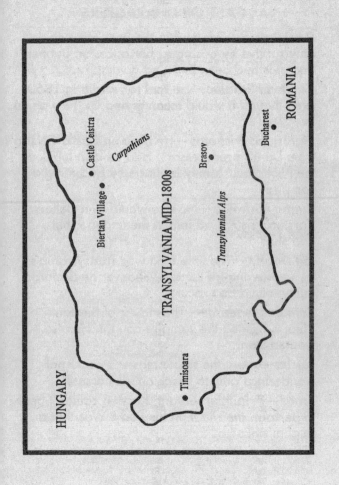

CAST OF CHARACTERS

Dani Patton—Trapped in the past, she could only survive by posing as her ancestor. But her ancestor had been branded a vampire.

Karsten Nicholae—He had to remain in 1850, even though it would mean giving up the woman he loved.

Sigismund Nicholae—He'd stolen Castle Ceistra from Dani's predecessors. Had he also fulfilled the Nicholaes' family heritage by becoming a vampire?

Zanna Nicholae—No one would ever believe Karsten's sister had joined the undead. But had she?

Ion Dobrin—The little man was Transylvania's foremost vampire hunter. Whoever he declared guilty would be executed.

Romulus Teodescu—The mayor of Biertan Village wanted the vampire caught. He also wanted Dani.

Letcha—Were the stable master's nocturnal wanderings *only* to check on his horses?

Ernos—A faithful servant, Karsten couldn't bear to perform *the ritual* on his body. Was that a fatal mistake?

Chapter One

All had looked. None had touched, except to bring her from the castle. To lay hands on her was courting death.

The man raised his gaze from her sleeping form and turned to the others. "We are as one, then? She is a vampire?"

Low murmurs of agreement answered him.

He looked over toward the fireplace, where a length of white thornwood was being carved in the light of the flames. "As soon as the stake is ready, bring it to me. The ritual must proceed."

He extended his hands, palms up, and waited.

TOUR GUIDES grew used to waking up in strange surroundings, but instinct told her these were stranger than most.

She was lying on something hard and flat, and her senses were warning her this was a hostile place—a place where people meant to harm her.

Fighting the impulse to bite her bottom lip—a childhood habit she reverted to under stress—she pretended she was still asleep and tried to remember what had happened earlier.

She'd gone to Castle Ceistra at dusk, just before closing time. Why hadn't she waited until morning, though?

Then, after she'd arrived . . .

Her brain was strangely groggy, and she couldn't force the details to surface. But she was no more in the castle now than she was safely home in San Diego. The smells and sounds weren't right for the castle. In fact, they were unfamiliar enough to be fear-inspiring all on their own.

A heavy, pungent odor hung in the air, so strong that it was burning deep in her throat. A vegetable smell, but acrid, not at all the reassuring aroma of home cooking.

Garlic. That was it. But far more pervasive than she'd ever smelled before.

There was smoke as well . . . perhaps from smoldering wood in a fireplace.

Yes, when she listened carefully, she could hear a fire quietly spitting. And she could make out the scent of melted wax . . . candles burning. Ale, as well. Mingled with the garlic and smoke, she was sure she detected a pub smell.

Then the murmur of a man's voice sent fresh fear rushing through her. Her heart began to race, its rhythm pounding in her ears, making it difficult to hear his words.

The voice sounded foreign, yet strangely familiar.

She couldn't figure out why for a minute. Then she realized he wasn't speaking English. It was Székely, the

Slavic dialect of her ancestry—the language she'd learned at her grandmother's knee.

Still keeping her face a mask of sleep, she tried to understand what the man was saying.

She couldn't. Székely took more concentration than English, and the hammering of her heart was making concentration impossible.

Then a different man, his voice coming from directly above her, began to intone a chant.

Gathering all her courage, she opened her eyes a tiny crack. She was in a cavernous, dim room, lit only by the candles she'd smelled. And she was lying on what felt like a long wooden table.

The man standing over her continued to chant, his arms raised above his head. His clothes were dirty and tattered, but a beautiful silver crucifix hung around his neck.

She risked opening her eyes a little more and could see the dark shapes of other people scattered around in the gloom. Twenty or so. But they were all watching from a distance. Only the man with the crucifix was standing close to her.

Her gaze followed his arms upward. Then her heart all but stopped.

In his hands he held an enormous wooden stake, its point aimed directly at her heart.

She tried to move but was paralyzed by terror.

The man raised his hands even further, readying himself to plunge the stake into her.

Frozen in place, she closed her eyes tightly, knowing death was imminent.

Suddenly, a deep male voice boomed across the room. "No! Stop!" a man roared in Székely. "I will not allow this!"

Her eyes flew open.

A dark figure swooped out of the darkness toward her. Momentarily, her horrified mind identified it as an enormous bat.

The next instant she realized it was really a man. His *wings* were actually a flowing black cloak, its cowl concealing his face. His *claws* were only his fingers in black leather gloves.

"'Tis the count's youngest son," someone whispered. "'Tis Karsten. We should have expected this."

The man swept her up into his arms and ordered everyone aside.

Vaguely, she realized she was wearing something unfamiliar over her sweater and jeans. She was wrapped in a long black wool cloak, much like his.

Then her attention focused entirely on the ominous way people began to mutter when the man started for the door with her.

They drew back into the shadows as he carried her past them, but the muttering grew rapidly angrier.

Ignoring them, he strode outside and hoisted her onto a black stallion.

She swung one leg across the horse's bare back, trying to quell a new fear. Being snatched from the jaws of a bizarre death was all well and good, but what if her rescuer had more in mind than just rescuing her?

For half a second, she considered sliding down off the horse. Then she looked over at the ancient tavern they'd just left and stopped considering.

No one had ventured after them, but several people were peering out—including the man with the stake. And regardless of what this dark horseman had in mind, it couldn't be worse than having a stake driven through her heart.

He'd unhitched the reins and leapt up behind her, saying, "Let's go, Ebony."

The animal took off like the wind, its mane whipping at her face, just as her hair had to be whipping at the man.

The man. Who was he? The count's youngest son, someone had said. Karsten.

His name meant nothing to her, but he'd saved her life. And even though he still hadn't said a word to her, his arms were around her, and her back was pressed against the reassuring breadth of his chest.

They raced along beneath the stars, the harvest moon bathing everything in gold. The September night was heavenly fresh after the stale air of the tavern, and snowcapped mountains glittered all around them in the moonlight.

She took a deep breath, finally daring to believe she wasn't going to die.

There were no sounds of pursuit, only the rhythmic thunder of Ebony's hooves carrying them away from the village and into the enveloping night.

In her terror she hadn't recognized it immediately, but it was Biertan Village they'd been in—a hamlet nestled in a valley of the Carpathians. It had been forgotten for centuries and was almost untouched by the passage of time.

In fact, tonight it had looked as if it hadn't been touched *at all* by time. Obviously there'd been some problem with the electricity.

Once she realized it was Biertan Village, she knew they weren't far from Castle Ceistra. So she'd been taken from the castle to a tavern in the village because...? By...?

A hundred questions were begging for answers, but she couldn't ask them—not while she was hurtling through the night on a galloping horse in the company of a dark stranger.

Finally, her rescuer reined Ebony off the road and onto a stretch of grass.

Dismounting, his face still hidden by the cowl of his cloak, he reached up, spanned her waist with his hands and lifted her down. As he did, a wolf howled in the distance.

The sudden, lonely call sent a shiver up her spine.

"It's all right, Danica," the man murmured. "You're safe now."

He'd called her by name, but how could he know it? And nobody except her grandparents called her Danica. To everyone else, she was Dani.

She gazed at him in uncertain silence, still not able to see his face. Then she carefully thought through the phrasing in Székely and asked, "Where are you taking me?"

"Back to Castle Ceistra, of course. You'll be safest there, with my family."

With my family. The phrase echoed uneasily in her mind. Nobody lived in Castle Ceistra. The Romanian Ministry of Tourism operated it as an historic site.

"But even there, Danica..." The man hesitated, then wrapped his arms tightly around her and drew her to him.

Her impulse to fight him came and went in the same heartbeat. Strange as it might seem, being in his arms felt right. And the strength of his body against hers was reassuring rather than frightening.

"My God, Danica," he whispered. "My God, why did you risk returning to Transylvania so soon? You should have stayed in Walachia. Didn't you realize they'd try to kill you?"

KARSTEN WAS LETTING Ebony move at a slow gait, so the horse could choose his footing carefully on the rocky mountain road.

The slower pace gave Dani plenty of time to think, although she was far from sure she wanted to think at all. She'd managed to calm down after they'd left Biertan Village behind, but now, the more she thought about things, the more incredible her suspicions became. As memories of the early evening gradually returned, her anxiety level was creeping higher and higher.

There were still foggy patches, but she thought she knew what had happened. Impossible as it was to believe, it seemed the only explanation that would account for Karsten's mention of Walachia.

She'd remembered about the portrait first, about why she'd gone to the castle on her own.

Parts of Castle Ceistra had still been under restoration when she'd brought the August Castle Tour group through. The library hadn't been open to the public. Now it was restored, though, she hadn't wanted to wait until morning to see it with her September tour group.

Way back, generations before her grandparents had emigrated to California, Castle Ceistra had belonged to her ancestors. The decor of the restored library was to include a portrait of the last member of her family to own it—Danica Radulesco, the woman she'd been named after.

So, as soon as she'd gotten her group checked into their hotel, Dani had quickly changed into casual clothes, then gone to the castle.

Once she'd reached the library, she'd been so excited at seeing the portrait that she hadn't even bothered reading about the newly opened room. She'd simply stuffed the information sheet into the pocket of her jeans and stood gazing at the painting.

It had given her such an eerie feeling that she'd been glad she was alone.

Dani bore a strong resemblance to her mother and grandmother, but gazing at the portrait was like gazing into a mirror.

It was a bridal portrait, and since Danica Radulesco had married in 1848, shortly before the revolution of 1848-49 had begun, she would have been only twenty-one at the time.

Dani Patton was twenty-eight but looked embarrassingly young. That made the age difference between her and the woman in the painting barely noticeable.

The overall resemblance was positively uncanny. True, Dani usually wore her dark hair loose, not sedately pulled back. But the dark brown eyes were the same, as was the pale skin, the high Slavic cheek-bones and the almost too-full mouth.

She'd stood behind the library's antique desk, staring intently at the portrait, until the lights had flicked off and on, warning that there were just ten minutes until closing.

Only then had she noticed the book on the desk.

It was an ancient book of spells, bound in rich burgundy leather and lying open, as if inviting her to read a few lines. And the crystal pyramid paperweight, resting on the open page, had seemed to be marking the place to begin. *The* place. The first line of a spell.

The harvest moon had just been rising, its golden light beginning to stream through the library's French windows.

Following the book's instructions, angling the crystal so it reflected the moonbeams, she'd read the spell aloud—even though she felt silly, knowing nothing at all would happen.

But suddenly, the room had grown dim and the portrait had vanished from the wall.

Seconds later, a man had appeared, looking like a butler who'd stepped out of the pages of history. He'd offered her tea, and then...that was where one of the foggy patches still remained.

Gazing ahead along the road, she tried to remember what had happened next. Then Ebony carried them around a curve and Castle Ceistra appeared.

Even with it before her, though, she couldn't be certain that her suspicions were founded in reality. That small thread of doubt let her cling to the hope that this entire experience was some sort of bizarre hallucination.

The stone wall surrounding the castle stretched as far as the eye could see at night, with just the turrets and crenulated battlements visible above it.

Of course, she could easily picture the entire enclosed area in her mind. Not only the gray stone Gothic castle that was the main residence, but also the outbuildings and stretches of gardens and trees.

Set on a large plateau, the property had been transformed over the centuries from barren rock into a tiny bucolic island. It was more like an English country estate than an East European fortress. Except, of course, for the sheer face of the mountain that protected it from behind.

Yes, she could easily picture everything that was enclosed within that stone wall. *Exactly* how was it going to look tonight, though?

Ebony trotted on, slowly carrying her closer and closer to the answer to that question.

The aroma of pine trees filled the air as they neared the open gate. Her first full glimpse inside the wall told her the impossible *had* to be true. The last faint hope that she was dreaming or hallucinating dissipated.

Even though a tiny, stubborn voice inside her head was still insisting that none of this could *possibly* be real, a far louder voice was pointing out that it was all too realistic to be merely a product of her subconscious.

Admitting to herself that the louder voice was right started her trembling.

"You're cold," Karsten murmured behind her. "Ernos should have given you a warmer cloak."

She didn't know who Ernos was, nor did she remember him giving her the cloak she was wearing.

Karsten brought the sides of his own cloak forward, wrapping them around her, then drawing her even more closely to him.

Feeling so shaky she was afraid she'd gone into shock, she pressed against Karsten's strength. But his comforting warmth couldn't stop her trembling, because her reaction had nothing to do with the cold—it was the result of this impossible thing that had happened.

There hadn't been a problem with the electricity back in Biertan Village, after all. There'd simply been no electricity. Similarly, there was no floodlit parking lot to the side of the castle and no floodlights illuminating the structure itself.

Old-fashioned blazing torches were mounted down either side of the grand stone entrance, throwing ominous, dancing shadows out into the pine trees that stood where the parking lot should have been. And what little light was visible inside the castle was so faint it had to be coming from candles or oil lamps.

This was what she'd been almost certain she'd see when they arrived. Still, it was incredibly difficult to accept.

Until tonight, she'd never believed in magic—not sorcery or wizardry or witchcraft or whatever else people chose to call it. Now, though, she wished with all her heart that she *had* believed. Because, if she had, she wouldn't have fooled with the occult for a second.

But she *had* fooled with it. And by playing with that crystal and reciting the spell, she'd sent herself back in time almost a century and a half, back to the time when Count Nicholae and his family had just moved into Castle Ceistra.

To be precise, she must have sent herself back to September 1850. The harvest moon assured her of the month, and Karsten had said, "Why did you risk returning to Transylvania *so soon?* You should have stayed in Walachia." And the woman he obviously thought she was, her great-great-great-great-great-grandmother, Danica Radulesco, had fled from Castle Ceistra to Walachia in October 1849.

AFTER THEY'D RIDDEN into the castle grounds, Karsten veered Ebony off the road and through the stand of pines. The bright moonlight scarcely penetrated their heavy growth, and the intense darkness did nothing for Dani's state of mind.

She *had* managed, though, to move from a state of panic to at least a semblance of self-control, which she was doing her best to maintain. The calmer she was, the better she'd be able to deal with this situation.

They rode maybe a hundred yards off to the left of the castle, then reached a moonlit clearing. Karsten reined Ebony in before the stone cottage that stood there.

"I'm going to put you in the groundkeeper's cottage for the night," he explained, dismounting. "You'll be fine unless...you aren't hungry, are you?"

"No. No, I'm fine."

"Good, because there's a problem with the stove. Nobody's been living in here lately, so we haven't bothered fixing it." Karsten reached to help her down as he finished speaking.

When her feet hit the ground, her legs felt like rubber. At one time, she'd ridden frequently, but it had been months since she'd been on a horse. Rubbery legs were at the bottom of her list of concerns, though, considering that she was in a century where she didn't belong and had barely escaped being killed.

When Karsten pushed back the cowl of his cloak, she gazed up at his face. The moonlight afforded her first clear look at him and revealed that he was about thirty, with strong, chiseled features and thick, pale hair pulled back into a ponytail. Probably the fashionable style for a count's son in 1850.

She'd been wondering about his relationship with Danica Radulesco, and his good looks made her even more curious. The way he'd hugged her, when they'd stopped to catch their breath outside Biertan Village, said he knew the woman he thought she was very well. But her ancestor had married another man, so she and Karsten must have been nothing more than friends.

"You'll be safer in the cottage," he said. "If the villagers get any more ideas tonight, they'll head straight for the castle."

"You really think they might come up here?" she asked, trying not to sound as terrified as she felt.

"They did earlier, didn't they? They came the minute Ernos sent down the message you were here."

"Ernos . . . sent a message?"

"Don't look so worried. He won't dare cause you any more trouble. When he told me what he'd done, I said I'd run him through if I didn't make it to the tavern in time."

"Ahh." So *that* was how Karsten had known she was in need of rescuing. She still wasn't positive who

Ernos was, but maybe he'd been the man who'd discovered her in the library, the one who'd brought her the tea.

"Karsten, I'm afraid I can't remember exactly what happened earlier. Even before I . . . fainted and all."

"You didn't faint. Ernos drugged you."

"The tea?"

Karsten nodded.

She waited anxiously for him to tell her more. If she could get answers without having to ask questions, it would be safer. Every time she opened her mouth, she was at risk of saying something she shouldn't.

"You really don't remember anything?" he asked at last.

"No. Almost nothing from the time I got to the castle until I woke up in the tavern."

"Well, you took Ernos by surprise. I think that's mostly what made him react the way he did. He didn't know how you'd gotten into the castle. So, naturally, he assumed you'd flown in through a window or something."

"Naturally," Dani murmured, smiling nervously. Whoever Ernos was, he had an awfully weird imagination. "Ahh...well...no one heard me knock and...I didn't mean to frighten him."

"No, of course not. But he was alone, so he *was* frightened. I mean, the other servants were there, but nobody with the strength to defend him against . . . well, you know."

"Ahh," she murmured again. She didn't know, but at least she had Ernos pegged for sure now.

So, she'd been drugged and almost sent to her death by a frightened servant. But why?

"I was out searching for...searching for some goats that had strayed," Karsten went on.

The sudden catch in his voice made Dani wonder if that was a lie. But why would he lie to her?

"And the rest of the family is away. My father and mother are spending a couple of months in Bucharest, and yesterday, Sigismund went off to...hunt. In the mountains."

"I see."

Sigismund. That was a name she recognized from her family's history. Sigismund was Count Nicholae's *eldest* son, and it was because of him that the Radulesco family had ultimately lost Castle Ceistra.

"At any rate," Karsten continued, "when Ernos suddenly saw you in the library, he panicked."

"He panicked," Dani repeated slowly, wondering what there was about her that would panic anyone. The way Karsten was eyeing her told her the question was written all over her face.

"Danica...don't you know what's been going on here? Didn't you receive my letter?"

She shook her head, almost tempted to tell him *why* she hadn't, to tell him that she wasn't actually Danica Radulesco.

Wasn't he bound to discover that for himself once he saw her in daylight? Of course, having seen the portrait, she knew that the family resemblance was astonishing. Plus, no one in Transylvania would have seen Danica Radulesco for almost a year. Still, he was likely to realize she was an impostor.

She didn't know what on earth she'd say if he did, but now didn't seem like a good time to try to explain the truth. Actually, she couldn't imagine there'd ever be a good time for *this* truth.

What would he think if she said that she'd come from a hundred and fifty years in the future? That she was really Danica *Patton,* the great-great-great-great-great granddaughter of the woman he'd taken her for? If she tried that on him, he'd be certain to think she was insane.

"Then you've really heard nothing about what happened in Transylvania after you left?" he was asking. "About the rumors, I mean?"

"I . . . no, not really."

Karsten rubbed his jaw, looking uneasy. "Danica, after the revolution was put down, after Transylvania was officially abolished as a country, the Austrians started rumors about some of the families that had risen against them."

Dani tensed at his words and waited for him to go on. Her ancestors had been among those who'd risen against the occupying Austrians. Count Radulesco had served as a commander in the nationalist army, and his sons had all fought in it. In fact, they'd given their lives for their country. Every one of Danica's five brothers had died during the year of bloody fighting, and her husband had been killed near the end of it, as well—barely a year after their marriage.

The young widow had then moved back into Castle Ceistra to be with her mother. And, as was the custom, she'd reverted to using her father's name, because he was still alive and her husband was dead. After the revolution finally failed, though, Count Radulesco had been executed for his part in it.

That had been in October 1849. And having been warned that they were about to be executed as well, his wife and daughter fled the country.

Karsten had begun speaking again, and Dani focused her attention on his words. "These rumors about the families..." he said, "the Austrians knew that their saying we were no longer a country wasn't going to make us accept it. And they were afraid of the people coming together again—of another uprising. So, to keep them from trusting one another, they spread rumors that some of the nationalist families...like yours...were..."

"Were what?"

"Danica, why do you think the villagers were going to drive a stake through your heart? Why do you think the Boar's Head Tavern stank of garlic?"

"I...I don't know. I've been too frightened to think through everything."

"Well, they were going to kill you because the Austrians told them your father was a vampire—and that you're one, as well."

Chapter Two

Dani stared at Karsten, totally appalled. She was in an even worse mess than she'd realized.

Bad enough to be in 1850 and not be certain whether she could ever return to her own time. People believing she was a vampire made things even worse. People who had tried to *kill* her, and who would undoubtedly try again if they got the chance.

Well there was no way she'd give them the chance. She'd managed to get herself here, so there *had* to be a way to get herself back. And she had to determine what it was as fast as she could—tonight, if possible. After all, come morning there were going to be twenty-one Californians expecting their guide to be hustling them onto the tour bus.

She'd been shepherding them day and night since they'd left San Diego on their charter last week, and if she wasn't there to help them order breakfast in the morning...well, she hated to think of what her boss, back home at the Living History Tours office, would have to say.

Twenty-one pampered Californians, stranded in the middle of Transylvania without a guide to run interference in the language of the locals, would quickly become twenty-one extremely unhappy tourists.

Step one to getting back to them, she realized, was getting into the castle library where the crystal and book of spells were. But that would be tricky, considering Karsten wanted her to spend the night in this cottage. She glanced uneasily past him at the small structure, doubting it would really be much of a hiding place if the villagers were intent on finding her.

"Now do you understand what happened earlier?" he asked quietly. "Why Ernos was so frightened when he found you in the castle? Why the villagers took you to the tavern? They wanted time to decide if you actually were a vampire."

"And they obviously decided I was. But how could people think...?"

"Danica, you know how superstitious the peasants are in Transylvania—especially in this part of the country. And it's hardly surprising, is it. Not considering that Count Dracula lives only a few miles away. Even your father...well, I don't have to remind you what he thought about my own family."

"No, of course you don't." Her *father*. Karsten was talking about one of her great-grandfathers. The one preceded by *six* "greats." She had no idea what he'd thought, but, at this point, it could hardly matter.

"And recently," Karsten continued, "there've been a few bodies discovered in the area. Three, in the past three days, to be exact."

"Bodies?" she repeated, her voice squeaking a little on the word. "You don't mean bodies with puncture wounds in their necks...do you?"

Karsten nodded. "And Dracula's been out of the country. You remember, he always goes to Moscow for opera season. So there *is* another of the Un-Dead in the area, no doubt about it. But we haven't been able to determine who it is yet."

She tried to smile, praying Karsten would smile back, praying this was a morbid joke.

His lips didn't even twitch.

But vampires had never been for real. And Count Dracula was just a character Bram Stoker had created, wasn't he?

She didn't believe for a minute that... well, *maybe* there was a real person named Count Dracula, and *maybe* he did live nearby, but he certainly *hadn't* lived here for hundreds of years.

Oh, she knew her ancestors had believed vampires existed, as had most people in 1850 Transylvania. But that had been way back... way back now. Anxiously, she glanced at the cottage again, saying, "Karsten, would you mind terribly if I stayed in the castle rather than here? I don't think I want to be alone."

"You'll be safer here. It's really a better idea than your being in the castle. I'll bring you one of the dogs for protection if you'd like. But, look, I've got a surprise for you."

He unlocked the door, led her inside and began lighting candles.

While he did, she tried to relax with a little deep breathing.

BY THE TIME KARSTEN had the cottage glowing in candlelight, Dani had almost convinced herself everything was going to be fine.

Being left alone out here wouldn't be a serious problem, because it was late enough that whoever else lived in the castle should be asleep. That meant she just had to give Karsten time to go to bed, then she'd be able to get into that library again and get herself back to the future.

Karsten turned to her with a smile. "Well? What do you think?"

Rather astonishingly, given the circumstances, what she caught herself thinking was that he had a very appealing smile. But that wasn't what he was getting at, so she looked around, puzzled.

It was a rather ordinary old stone cottage, with a large fireplace in the living room. On one side was a door that she assumed led to a bedroom. On the other, there was a tiny alcove of a kitchen.

Her gaze lingered for a moment on the little potbellied, wood-burning stove. Karsten needn't have worried about her wanting to use it. She'd have been too frightened that she'd do something that would make it explode, even if he hadn't mentioned there was a problem with it.

She glanced around the main room once more. The candles lent it a warm, golden sheen, but there were still a lot of dark, spooky shadows. And she certainly hadn't missed the rustling sounds of mice scurrying for cover.

If she hadn't intended to leave right away, she'd have asked Karsten for a cat, in addition to that dog he'd mentioned bringing.

When she looked back at him, he was still smiling. He seemed to be expecting a major reaction from her about the accommodations. But why would he care what she thought of the groundkeeper's cottage?

"It's . . . very nice," she offered at last.

"Danica, don't you recognize your things?"

Her things? He meant Danica Radulesco's things, she realized after a second. It gave her a creepy feeling.

He was assigning her to someone else's life, and the idea was extremely unsettling. She wouldn't have liked it even if people *hadn't* believed the *someone else* was a vampire.

"When we moved into the castle," he was saying, "I had everything taken from your room and stored out here for you. Your clothes are in the wardrobe in the bedroom. My mother and Zanna organized them. Your jewelry is out here, too, but we left your mother's in the castle. We couldn't believe you'd both left behind so many valuable pieces."

"We had to leave very quickly . . . there just wasn't time for everything."

Karsten nodded. "And I put your diaries safely in a box. I knew how important they were to you."

He paused, then went on more hesitantly. "I brought out that portrait of you, too. The one your father had hanging in his library. But I wasn't sure . . . I hope it doesn't bring back too many painful memories."

"No. No, I'm glad it's here. It reminds me of the good times," she murmured, gazing at the bridal portrait on the far wall.

It probably *would* have brought back painful memories for Danica Radulesco, but Dani didn't even know the name of the man who'd so briefly been married to her ancestor.

"And I... of course I recognized everything," she lied, desperately trying to keep up her facade of calm while feeling anything but. "You just took me by surprise, Karsten. I wasn't expecting to see anything familiar in here. But thank you. Thank you so much for keeping it all safe."

He gave her an embarrassed shrug. "I knew you'd be coming back—eventually. And this thing with the castle...you must know how awkward I feel about it. But if my father hadn't agreed to take it over, someone else would have. Someone who might not have been willing to return it to you when the time came. You understand, don't you?"

"Yes, I understand," she said, glancing at the portrait once more. It might not bring back painful memories, but seeing it there made her very, very nervous.

This was the second time tonight she'd seen it. The first time had been in the castle, in the future. Now it was out here in this cottage, in the previous century.

That started her thinking about how incredibly complex the mechanics of time travel must be. What if they were so complicated that she wouldn't be able to get back to where she belonged?

She forced away the sense of panic that thought caused. She *was* going to get back.

But maybe, just in case she ended up stuck here for a day or so, she'd better establish exactly what was what. "Karsten?"

"Yes?"

She paused for a moment, gazing into the depth of his blue eyes. They had an almost mesmerizing effect. The candlelight made their soft blue as deep as the Adriatic, a blue you could lose yourself in.

Pulling her gaze away before that could happen, she said, "Karsten, if the villagers see me in the daylight tomorrow, everything will be fine, won't it?"

He looked at her blankly.

"I mean, everyone knows that vampires can't be out between sunrise and sunset, right? So if they see me during the daytime..."

Karsten's expression changed from blank to mystified. "Are you feeling unwell, Danica? We haven't believed that myth since we were children. You know the Un-Dead can be active anytime they like. Their only problem is that their powers are diminished by daylight."

"Their powers," she repeated uncertainly.

"Of course. They can't fly during the day. And they don't have nearly the strength they have at night. And they can only change into bats or wolves or mist after sunset. And... but you already know all this. What's got you confused?"

"I...I guess it's just been a long, frightening night. And that drug Ernos put in the tea. It made my mind so fuzzy I can still hardly think."

Karsten nodded, then slipped his cloak off and tossed it onto a chair. Crouching down in front of the fireplace, he began arranging wood for a fire.

She watched him, firmly telling herself not to worry. With any luck, she'd be gone from here in an hour or two. Then none of this vampire nonsense would be relevant.

The flickering light threw shadows against the straight lines of Karsten's profile and made his long hair seem even paler than it had looked in the moonlight. When he reached for a log, his white shirt stretched tightly across his back, drawing her attention to the breadth of his shoulders.

There was something about him—aside from his obvious good looks—that she found surprisingly attractive. Probably, she decided, it was the fact that he'd saved her life. Nothing like a man rescuing her from the jaws of death to make her appreciate him.

Looking away from Karsten and focusing on nothing, she thought about the story her grandmother told of how the Nicholaes had come to live in Castle Ceistra.

Before the revolution of 1848-49, they'd lived a short distance away. But when Count Nicholae refused to take part in the uprising, the revolutionaries had punished him by seizing his castle to use as one of their headquarters. By the end of the fighting, it was practically in ruins, virtually uninhabitable.

After the revolution was put down, and Danica and her mother had fled from Castle Ceistra, the Austrians rewarded the Count's neutrality by giving it to him to live in.

Dani glanced at Karsten again, wondering if he had been honest with her. Had his father really intended to give possession of Castle Ceistra back to Danica Radulesco when the time came?

According to her grandmother's story, the question had never arisen, because Danica never returned to Transylvania. And who could have blamed her, after all the tragedy that had befallen her family here?

In fact, it was close to twenty years before a Radulesco *did* attempt to reclaim the castle. Both Danica and her mother had died in Walachia, and Danica's claim to Castle Ceistra had passed to her daughter.

The girl eventually appeared, but old Count Nicholae was dead by then, and his eldest son, Sigismund, was firmly entrenched in the castle. He'd simply refused to pay any heed to the daughter's claim of ownership, and she'd eventually given up trying to plead her case.

Karsten pushed himself up off the floor and grabbed his cloak from the chair. "I'd better get Ebony to the stable. Letcha never turns in until all the animals have been tended to. You remember Letcha? The stable master?"

"I . . . I probably do. It's just the tea."

"Well, he'll certainly remember you. You and Zanna used to drive him crazy when you were children, always wanting to ride horses that were too big for you."

Dani managed a smile and mentally filed away the names—just in case she didn't get out of here as quickly as she was hoping.

Letcha was in charge of the stable. And that was the second time Karsten had mentioned the name Zanna. Earlier, he'd said that she'd helped his mother organize things in the cottage, so she was probably his sister.

"I'll be back in a few minutes," he said, pausing in the doorway. "And I'll bring you one of the dogs so you won't be alone."

THE DOG PROVED TO BE a borzoi, a Russian wolf-hound that was very elegant and aristocratic looking.

Dani stood in the cottage doorway, eyeing it un-happily. Greyhound thin, but with long silky white hair, it was absolutely beautiful. She'd have preferred something sturdy and mean-looking though—like a bullmastiff or a rottweiler.

"This is Czar," Karsten said, ushering the skinny dog inside.

"Ahh... Czar," she repeated, giving him a tenta-tive pat. He wasn't a small dog—his head reached her waist, but it was such a delicate, narrow head that there couldn't be much room in it for serious teeth. "And if anyone comes around the cottage, he'll...?"

"Bark."

"Bark. Good." She watched Czar wander over and gracefully curl up in front of the fireplace. He was, she decided, better than nothing.

If a vampire slayer showed up before she got out of here, at least she'd have a warning. And the barking might even frighten the fellow off—as long as he didn't see what a delicate dog was making the noise.

"I brought you this, as well," Karsten said, pro-ducing a revolver.

"Thank you. I hope I won't need it though." And, with any luck, she wouldn't. With any luck, she'd be inside that castle within the hour, then back in the twentieth century.

"You still have your cloak on," Karsten said. "Is it too cold in here? Would you like me to add some logs to the fire?"

"No, I'm fine. I just haven't gotten around to tak-ing it off." Actually, it would be disastrous to let him see the jeans and sweater she was wearing—not to mention the waist pack she always used on tours instead of a purse.

She'd been wondering what Ernos had thought when he'd seen the way she was dressed. She doubted Levi Strauss had exported to 1850 Transylvania. Besides, it had probably been unheard of for women to wear *any* kind of pants.

So maybe her strange outfit had helped convince Ernos she was a vampire. Or, perhaps, finding her in the library had frightened him so badly that he hadn't really noticed her clothes.

"In the morning," Karsten was saying, "we'll decide what you should do. But I think the obvious solution is for you to go back to Walachia until things have settled down here."

She nodded, although that wasn't a viable option. Not even if—horror of horrors—she ended up stuck in the past. The Danica who belonged in 1850 was already in Walachia.

"Well...good night," Karsten said, his hand on the door.

"Good night, Karsten. And thank you... for rescuing me... for keeping my things safe... for everything."

He gave her the same sort of embarrassed shrug he'd given earlier when she'd thanked him, then turned quickly away.

Dani watched him stride off into the darkness. If she *did* get back to where she belonged tonight, she'd never see him again. And crazy as it might seem, that prospect made her a little sad. There was something very appealing about his old-fashioned gallantry.

She smiled to herself at the thought. It was hardly surprising that he seemed old-fashioned to her. But surely, even in 1850, not every nobleman in Transylvania would have come riding to her rescue like a Slavic Sir Galahad.

Karsten disappeared into the pines without a backward glance. She slowly closed the door, musing that, in her world, there was a desperate shortage of heroes.

Cautiously, assuming old guns discharged easily, she put the one he'd given her into the pocket of the cloak. She was almost as worried about it going off accidentally as she was about the possibility of having to use it.

She stood watching the fire dance in the fireplace for a little while, anxious to get started but wanting to give Karsten enough time to settle in for the night.

At last, unable to stand the wait any longer, she headed back over to the door.

Czar scrambled to his feet and she hesitated. She wouldn't mind his company, walking through that dark stand of trees between the cottage and the castle, but she couldn't risk the chance that he might bark and alert someone.

"You stay here, boy," she murmured, giving him a farewell scratch behind the ear. Then she slipped quietly out, firmly closing the door on him.

With her cloak hiked up so it wouldn't trail on the ground, her heart anxiously pounding, she stole through the pines, trying to ignore the unfamiliar noises of the night.

A sudden rustling of leaves started her adrenaline pumping. An owl's hoot made her heart skip a beat.

But when she reached the far edge of the trees, all was quiet.

The castle stood in darkness. The torches that had lit the front entrance earlier had been extinguished and there was no visible light inside. Beyond that, where she knew from her tours that the stable stood, all was quiet and dark as well.

She stole silently across the cobblestones, glad of the rubber soles on her sneakers. Then, as she headed around the side of the castle to the library windows, she reached beneath her cloak and dug a credit card out of her waist pack.

Not that she had any experience as a break-and-enter artist, but she knew that French windows often didn't have very secure locks. Slipping the card into the crack between the two windows, she angled it the way she'd seen people do a thousand times on TV.

It promptly slipped back out again.

Her next few tries were just as unsuccessful. But finally, palms sweating, her effort was rewarded with a click and the latch slid out of place.

Barely breathing, she pulled the windows open and climbed into the library. The moonlight was bright enough that she easily located wooden matches to light the oil lamp on the desk.

The quivering flame immediately danced its light onto the crystal pyramid paperweight, making it glitter. But the book of spells wasn't lying where she'd last seen it.

For one panicky second, she stared blankly at the surface of the desk. Then she realized what the problem was.

That book had been placed on the desk in the future—an interesting prop, a finishing touch after the library had been restored. But it wouldn't have been lying there, open, in 1850.

Praying it had actually belonged in the old castle library, that the decorator hadn't just bought it a few months ago in a used bookstore, she turned to the bookshelves behind her and began methodically moving the lamp along them, searching for a thick book with burgundy leather binding.

When she eventually spotted it, she almost sagged with relief. She pulled it down from its spot on the shelf, put it and the lamp on the desk, and began flipping through the pages, looking for the spell.

It had been somewhere near the middle...and there it was—the spell that had gotten her into this mess.

Her eyes flashed to the bottom of it and a chorus of hallelujahs erupted in her head. The spell directly following it *was* a reverse one. She'd *thought* she'd noticed that earlier, but hadn't been certain because she hadn't read it very closely. Never in a million years would she have believed she'd be needing a spell to get herself back to the future. But, then again, who would have thought that the one she'd tried would have actually transported her to the past?

Carefully picking up the crystal, she read the first few words of the reverse spell. And then her heart dropped all the way to her toes.

The first spell, loosely translated into English, had begun, "Only on the night of a harvest moon..."

But this one started, "Only on the night of a hunter's moon..."

What on earth was a hunter's moon? She had no idea. But whatever it was, it wasn't a harvest moon, which was the moon high overhead in the sky tonight, and which had been critical to the success of the first spell.

Frantically, she grabbed the lamp and turned back to the bookcase. There was a multivolume encyclopedia, and she pulled down the appropriate volume.

Opening it, she checked under the Székely word for *hunter*. There was nothing except a few biographies of men by that name.

She grabbed another volume and quickly flipped to the translation for *harvest,* hoping both moons might be listed under that, but there was nothing at all about moons.

She could feel panic threatening again and told herself to calm down. There was still *moon* to try. Almost afraid to look, she found the entry and trailed her finger down it, through the old scientific data about size and orbit, until she reached a section titled "Phases of the Moon."

Sure enough, there was a little subsection titled "Harvest Moon and Hunter's Moon." Slowly, she began reading:

> *The harvest moon, the full moon nearest the autumnal equinox, ushers in a period of successive days when the moon rises soon after sunset. This phenomenon gives farmers extra hours of light in which to harvest their crops before frost and winter.*

Right. She'd known the harvest moon was a full moon in September.

She read on:

The next full moon, known as the hunter's moon, is accompanied by a similar phenomenon, although less marked.

The next full moon? The reverse spell, the one that could get her back to the future, would only work on the night of *October's* full moon?

October? The full ghastliness of the situation wiggled its way into her mind. Even if she could ultimately make the reverse spell work, she was going to be stuck in 1850 for an entire month.

So much for getting back to her tour. In fact, so much for her job. When her group found she was gone, one of them would get on the phone to California, and her boss would have a fit.

The brass at Living History Tours would never believe she'd gotten stuck in the wrong century. They'd be certain she'd just deserted her group.

But getting fired, she quickly realized, was the least of her worries. Her parents would be absolutely frantic when they learned she'd vanished into the night. By the time a month had passed, they'd be sure she was dead.

And as far as she, herself, was concerned, only a few miles away there was a village full of people who thought she was a vampire.

She began to bite nervously on her bottom lip—that old childhood stress reaction. But she had no more than a few seconds to worry about her predicament before she heard noises that made her heart start racing and her mouth go dry.

Muffled, scuffling sounds were coming from directly outside the library door. Someone, or more than one someone, was in the hallway. The noises startled her so badly that she bit into her lip—hard enough to draw blood—and barely managed to keep from crying out in pain.

She quickly blew out the lamp and ducked behind the desk, trying to think past the fear that was threatening to freeze her brain.

Karsten had told her the castle wouldn't be a safe place for her. Had some of the villagers actually ridden up here? Had some of them gotten inside?

Anxiously, she licked the blood from her lip, ignoring its salty taste in her mouth and trying to decide what to do.

If whoever was out there was after her, hiding behind a desk probably wouldn't save her.

Pushing herself up far enough to see through the open windows, she weighed her options. If she tried to make it back to the cottage, and there were villagers with murderous intent out there...

As much as she didn't like being in here, she didn't like the possibility of being caught outside in the bright moonlight any better.

She realized that the noises in the hall seemed to have stopped and listened intently, barely breathing.

Only the ticking of the pendulum clock in the corner broke the silence. Each second that ticked away seemed like an hour, but there were no further sounds from beyond the room.

Still not entirely certain what she should do, she looked outside again.

A tiny chill seized her. Just disappearing from her field of vision, heading in the direction of the stable, was a dark figure shrouded in a cloak.

That made her decision simple. There was no way she was going back out through the window at the moment.

Cautiously, she drew the gun out of her cloak pocket and crept across to the door. Pausing there, she listened carefully again, gave her bloody lip another lick, and then slowly turned the handle.

She didn't see the dark shape lying on the hallway floor until she tripped over it. And when that happened, her heart leaped to her throat.

The shape was a body.

She stared down at it, terrified, unable to make out if it was a man or a woman.

An impulse told her to flee, while a contradictory one told her to stay and find out what was going on.

Gazing along the hallway into the darkness, she decided there was definitely no one else there. Then she hurried back to the desk.

Hands trembling, she put the gun into her pocket once more and relit the lamp. Her knees trembling at least as badly as her hands, she carried the lamp into the hall and knelt beside the body.

It was a man, facedown on the carpet.

She put the lamp onto the floor, screwed up all her nerve and rolled him over onto his side.

Chapter Three

The scream cut through Karsten's sleep like a knife. He grabbed his revolver and was halfway to the staircase before the sound fully died.

How long had he been asleep? Seconds? Minutes? Hours?

He'd lain down on the bed, still fully dressed, lost in his thoughts about Danica's unexpected arrival. The next thing he'd known, the scream had wakened him.

"Karsten?" his sister called from the darkness behind him. "Karsten, what's happening?"

"Get back in your room, Zanna," he shouted over his shoulder. "Lock the door and stay there."

He pounded down the stone staircase and raced blindly in the direction of the library, certain that was where the scream had come from.

Sounds of frightened voices were drifting out of the servants' wing, but no one appeared.

As he started along the hallway leading to the library, he noticed a faint light ahead—a lamp on the floor, a dark form beside it.

He stopped in his tracks, realizing the form was a person. Then, looking more carefully, he saw there were two people. One was crumpled in a heap. The second was on its knees, hunched over the crumpled one.

The flickering light from the lamp was creating grotesque, monsterlike shadows of them on the wall.

Unable to make out who they were or what they were doing, Karsten began creeping forward, his gun at the ready.

Then his boot made a scuffling noise against the stone floor, and the kneeling person whirled toward him.

"Oh, my God," he murmured as the light fell across her face.

Danica was staring at him wide-eyed. Tears streaming down her cheeks. Her mouth wet with blood.

"He's dead," she whispered, brushing fiercely at the tracks of her tears. "Karsten, he's dead."

Feeling sick, Karsten tucked his gun into his waistband, then reached past her for the lamp. The coppery scent of blood and death hovered above the body.

"Ernos," he murmured when the light spilled over the servant, revealing his identity.

The man's face was a deathly, bloodless shade. And Karsten knew, even before he turned Ernos's head to the side, what he'd see.

Sure enough, there were two telltale puncture marks on his neck. They were still oozing blood.

"Karsten?" Danica whispered.

He looked at her again, crouched beside the body like a she-wolf. Even in the faint lamplight, the wet blood glistened on her lips. The sight of it turned his stomach—it was all he could do to choke down his horror.

Danica. He'd known her forever. She'd tagged along after him and her brothers when she was little. How could she have come to such a fate?

He put the lamp back on the floor. Then, only too aware of what he had to do, he drew his gun once more.

Ever since the first body had been found three days ago, he'd been searching for the vampire, so he was prepared for it. He'd melted down silver to make the bullets his revolver was loaded with. And upstairs was a stake he'd carved of the finest white thornwood. But he'd never imagined it would be Danica he'd be using them on.

When he cocked his gun the click drew her attention.

She looked at him, absently rubbing the back of her hand across her mouth. Then she sat staring at the blood she'd wiped from her lips, her expression confused.

"Oh, no," she whispered after a second, her eyes flashing to his. "Oh, no, Karsten, you can't be thinking..."

"Danica, how could it have happened to you?"

"No! I bit my lip. I was startled and...please, look at it. Ernos was dead when I found him. And this blood...this is *my* blood. I swear it is. Just look."

Pressing her fingers to her bottom lip, she gazed beseechingly at him.

His heart was thudding against the wall of his chest. What if she was trying to trick him into getting too close? And then...

"Karsten?" she whispered. "Please believe me. If *you* don't, no one will."

He eyed her a moment, then hesitantly reached forward and pulled her lower lip down with his thumb.

"It's cut," she whispered. "Can you see that it's bleeding?"

He nodded slowly, suddenly less certain he knew what had happened. But she might have bitten her lip intentionally, trying to throw him off.

"Karsten, listen to me," she said as he drew his hand away. "There was something I had to check in a book. It couldn't wait until morning, so I came in through the library window. Then I heard noises out here in the hall. And after they'd stopped I . . . and he was just lying here. With those . . . those *marks* on his neck. And when I saw them, I screamed."

Karsten tried to think clearly. If she *had* killed Ernos, the last thing she would have done was scream. Wakening the entire castle made no sense. So could she possibly be telling the truth?

"Karsten?" Zanna called from the darkness of the hallway behind them.

"Who's that?" Danica whispered, her words sounding terrified.

"My sister. Why are you asking when you know her voice better than mine?" He grabbed Danica by the hand and pulled her up off the floor. If *Zanna's* curiosity had overcome her fear, the servants would be along any minute, too.

"Zanna," he shouted, "get back upstairs. Everything is going to be fine, just get back to your room now. That goes for everyone. I want you all to stay in your rooms for the rest of the night."

The scuffling of several pairs of feet told him it definitely hadn't been only Zanna coming to investigate.

"Get in the library," he whispered to Danica. "Take the lamp with you."

She scooped it up off the floor so fast the flame blew out, and she raced from the hall like a frightened rabbit.

Karsten tucked his gun away, then dragged Ernos's body into the library. Locking the door, he turned to Danica.

She was standing in the moonlight, staring at the body—her face pale as death—looking as if she were about to start crying once more.

Behind her, on the desk, lay several books. And behind the desk, the windows stood ajar. So, had she really come into the castle to look something up? Maybe Ernos had discovered her and she'd killed him so that he couldn't tell anyone he'd seen her. Is that how events had unfolded?

But the facts didn't quite add up. Despite what Karsten had thought when he'd seen that blood on her mouth, the idea of Danica being a vampire... and he just couldn't make her scream fit in.

If she *had* killed Ernos, why wouldn't she have slipped quietly back out the way she'd come in? But if she *hadn't* killed him, who had?

Was the vampire one of the castle residents? Or had someone broken in?

"Karsten?"

He glanced at Danica.

"I saw someone outside, earlier, before I found the body. It was a few minutes after the noises stopped in the hallway. Someone wearing a cloak—a man, I thought—was hurrying away from the castle in the direction of the stable. Do you think it might have been . . . ?''

"A vampire wouldn't *walk* away, Danica. It would vanish in a mist. Or fly off as a bat. Or run away as a wolf. It was probably Letcha you saw."

"In the middle of the night?"

"He sometimes has trouble sleeping, and when he does he often goes to check on the animals."

"Isn't that a little . . . peculiar?"

"I guess. But you know Letcha."

The moonlight suddenly dimmed, and Karsten glanced out the window. A mist hung in the air for a moment, then dissipated before his eyes.

It sent a chill through him. As he'd just said, vampires didn't *walk* away after they'd killed. They did often travel as mist, though.

He looked at Danica again, knowing he needed time to figure things out. Time without her watching him, her deep brown eyes protesting her innocence.

"Karsten?"

"What?"

"You *do* believe it wasn't me, don't you?"

"I don't know," he said honestly. "But let's get you back to the cottage. Then I'll decide what to do."

KARSTEN CLIMBED BACK in through the library window and sank into the chair behind the desk. A glance assured him that the door was still safely locked. No one had been in the room, and the castle was quiet. He had time to think now.

He absently rubbed his jaw, trying to organize his thoughts. Danica hadn't told him the entire truth. When he'd asked her what she'd been trying to find in the library, what had been so important it couldn't wait till morning, her answer had been evasive and hadn't made much sense.

But not telling him the entire truth hardly proved she was a vampire—and he'd rather not think that was even a possibility.

He knew it was, though. Anyone could join the ranks of the Un-Dead. They could either be recruited by force, or they could choose eternal existence if it was offered. All it took was drinking a vampire's blood immediately after he drained your body. Three days later, you'd have changed into a vampire.

And there was no denying that Danica had somehow changed. She seemed almost a different person from the woman who'd left Transylvania a year ago.

After all she'd been through, losing most of her family and her husband, that was hardly surprising. But he couldn't pinpoint exactly *how* she'd changed.

Strangely enough, whatever the difference was, it seemed to have affected his reactions to her.

She'd always been much the same as Zanna to him, almost like another sister. But tonight, he hadn't felt the least bit brotherly. Instead, he'd found being close to Danica disconcerting.

The entire night, though, had been disconcerting.

He looked over toward the door again, at the dark shape of Ernos's body still lying on the floor. When he'd seen Danica crouched beside it earlier, blood on her mouth, he'd really thought she'd murdered the man. In that instant, he'd decided she must have returned from Walachia a few days ago, before the recent series of killings had begun, and that Ernos had just become her fourth victim.

In that instant, everything had seemed perfectly clear. Now, nothing seemed clear.

He simply couldn't make himself believe there was anything evil about Danica. So, now he had to decide what to do with Ernos's body. If he wanted to keep Danica from coming to harm, no one could see it until after the real Un-Dead was found.

Everyone knew Danica was here. Where else would he have taken her? And if they learned Ernos had been killed, they'd be even more certain that she was a vampire. That would make them want to tear her apart.

Glancing at the body once more, his throat tightened. He knew he should perform the ritual—to be on the safe side—but he wasn't sure he could bring himself to do it.

Ernos had been a good and loyal servant, and the idea of driving a stake through his heart, then slicing off his head and stuffing his mouth with garlic, was totally repugnant.

But what if Ernos had drunk of the vampire's blood before dying? If he had, and the proper precautions weren't taken, he'd become one of the Un-Dead himself.

Karsten lit the lamp, then pulled out his pocket watch and checked the time. It was already almost four. He was lucky this wasn't a night when he'd been expected elsewhere hours ago.

Leaning back in the chair, he sat trying to think of a solution to his problem—one that wouldn't involve desecrating Ernos's body. Then, in the flickering lamplight, he absently glanced at the books Danica had been looking at.

They were still lying on the desk. Three were volumes of the encyclopedia. Even if he looked through them, he'd never be able to figure out what she'd been checking. And the fourth was a book of magic spells.

He stared at that for a minute, uneasily wondering if vampires used spells. As far as he knew, they didn't. But witches did—and to the villagers' minds, killing witches was almost as important as killing vampires.

Until he got Danica safely on her way back to Walachia, he'd have to keep a close eye on her. At least he would if he wanted to ensure she'd be safe...if he wanted to ensure *everyone* would be safe.

Like it or not, he couldn't be entirely certain Danica *wasn't* the vampire. And if she was, and she killed again now that he'd let her live, he'd be responsible.

Wearily, he ran his fingers through his hair. The sooner she left the better, because how could he watch what she was up to and continue his vampire hunting at the same time?

And he *did* have to keep hunting.

Generations before the Austrians had circulated the recent vampire rumors about the revolutionary families, similar rumors had existed about the Nicholae family. And, every so often, they resurfaced.

That was why he and Sigismund had been out searching for the vampire ever since the first body had been discovered.

The longer there was one of the Un-Dead roaming the area, the more people would reflect on those old

rumors, and the more they'd convince themselves that
the Nicholaes really did have a vampire heritage.

Soon, if the Un-Dead wasn't stopped, the villagers
would be readying stakes for every member of his
family.

WHEN DAYLIGHT CREPT into the cottage, Czar demanded to be let out.

Dani closed the door behind him and returned to the
couch. It had taken her the entire night, but she'd
reached the last entry in the final volume of Danica
Radulesco's diaries.

Dated October 7, 1849, it read:

We have received word that Father was executed
yesterday at Arad, along with other commanders
of the defeated nationalist army. Tomorrow,
mother and I must flee the castle as we have been
warned of plans to kill us, as well.

Mother says we cannot carry many belongings
with us, but I will begin a new journal on the trip,
as I will begin a new life.

I would almost rather die, and thus be united
with my father and brothers once more. And
most of all, be with my beloved husband. But I
must go on because I am with his child and must
live for her.

I know it will be a daughter, but have told no
one about her yet. If Mother knew, she would
worry about me should the trip to Walachia prove
difficult. I pray it will not. I fear we cannot survive much more hardship.

There were stains on the final page that Dani was sure were dried tears, and she wiped away a few tears of her own.

One by one, the last year's entries had told of the deaths of Danica Radulesco's brothers, killed in the fighting. They also described the heartbreaking death of her young husband. Then, finally, there was the tragic news of her father's execution.

Dani had already known the facts of her family's history, but her ancestor's words made each death individual and real, eliciting a far more emotional response than the simple facts ever had.

Little wonder Danica and her mother had left so much of value behind. They must have been so emotionally wrung out that they hadn't cared at all about material things.

Blinking back fresh tears, Dani closed the little book. Even though the diaries had left her feeling sad, reading them had been the best thing she could possibly have done.

She'd learned all kinds of potentially useful details about the Radulesco family. And, most important, she felt she knew the woman in that portrait on the wall.

The question was, did she know her well enough to become her for an entire month?

The more she'd thought about it, passing as Danica Radulesco seemed the only way to survive long enough to greet the hunter's moon. She just couldn't think of any way to explain the truth about who she was without sounding crazy. Her being here was so unbelievable that even she had trouble accepting it.

And if people decided she was crazy...well, back in 1850, they burned lunatics at the stake in this part of the world.

She gazed absently through the window, not feeling particularly frightened about being alone now that it was morning. The only thing she felt really frightened about was being stuck in 1850...and about all those people in Biertan Village who were convinced she was a vampire...and about Ernos having been killed last night—or, more accurately, about *who* or *what* had killed him.

She knew only one person in 1850. And after some of the things she'd read about Karsten's family in those diaries...

Of course, she didn't *really* believe in vampires any more than she believed in magic spells. At least, any more than she *hadn't* believed in magic spells before she'd gotten herself stuck in the wrong century.

Now that she'd actually traveled through time, though, should she be doubting *anything?* Possibly, even the disturbing story about the Nicholaes had some truth to it.

Danica Radulesco obviously hadn't believed it. But according to local legend, one Nicholae in each generation converted to vampirism. There was always one who *chose* to take the dark gift from an ancestor.

These Un-Dead ancestors, according to the story, lived together in a Nicholae vampire coven someplace. Eventually, each generation's vampire went off to live with the others. That, the explanation went, was why people could never *prove* any one of them lived on forever.

Dani slowly shook her head, no longer certain what she should believe. The only thing she knew for sure was that somebody was murdering people by draining their blood. So, if vampires weren't for real, then there was a serial killer on the prowl. She'd seen *Silence of the Lambs,* so she knew serial killers often did bizarre things to their victims.

But regardless of who or what had left those gruesome marks on Ernos's neck...well, unless it was some mysterious stranger, the most likely suspect was somebody who lived in Castle Ceistra. And the more she thought about Karsten's quick appearance after she'd found the body, the more she wondered why he'd still been fully dressed.

She'd assumed he'd be in bed, asleep, before she'd gone in through that library window. Instead, maybe he'd been right outside in the hall, killing Ernos.

But *Karsten?* Biting necks and drinking blood? The thought made her shiver.

She really didn't want the only person she knew in 1850 to be either a vampire *or* a serial killer. She really, really didn't.

Anxiously, she rubbed her hands along her thighs and realized she was still wearing her jeans. She'd meant to check out that wardrobe full of Danica Radulesco's things hours ago, but she'd gotten too engrossed in the diaries.

She quickly headed into the bedroom. If anyone saw her dressed the way she was, they'd realize she was an impostor in a second. The thought sent another shiver through her. She suspected they burned impostors, as well as lunatics, at the stake.

With that in mind, she took off her watch, carefully checked that the alarm on it wasn't set, then tucked it away in her waist pack.

The alarm was a godsend when tour buses were collecting her groups early in the morning, but the last thing she needed was to have it accidentally go off here.

She pulled open the wardrobe doors and was greeted by the scent of a cedar lining. A row of dresses hung neatly before her. Above that was a shelf for hats, below it, a ledge for shoes. In a special little compartment that she almost overlooked, she discovered a jewelry case.

When she opened it the contents took her breath away. The pieces were beautiful—mostly diamonds and emeralds. If they were real, and they certainly looked it, Karsten hadn't been exaggerating their value last night—they had to be worth a fortune.

Carefully putting the case back where it belonged, she looked through the section of drawers on the right-hand side of the wardrobe. They contained everything else she'd need.

Well, *almost* everything.

After rifling through the lingerie drawer twice, she decided she'd be rinsing out her silk panties and comfortable sports bra every night. There were limits to how authentic her impersonation was going to be. She had no intention of starting to wear corsets and coarse cotton bloomers—not when absolutely nobody but her would be seeing what she had on under Danica Radulesco's dresses.

Feeling like a little girl getting ready for Halloween, she peeled off her own clothes and put on a long blue wool dress. It was a perfect fit.

All the shoes she tried, though, were a little large. She'd have to remember not to walk too fast, or she'd walk right out of them.

She tossed her sneakers into the recesses of the wardrobe, thinking she'd been lucky that the long cloak had covered them last night. They'd never pass as 1850's shoes.

Then, fully dressed, she gazed at herself in the mirror on the wardrobe door. All of a sudden, a wonderful thought struck her. Vampires didn't reflect in mirrors. If she showed people she had a reflection, they'd stop thinking she was a vampire. Unless...

She might be entirely wrong about the reflection thing. Just as she'd been wrong in thinking vampires couldn't wander around in the daylight.

Last night, Karsten had bought her explanation that she'd simply gotten confused about vampire lore because of that drugged tea. But if she paraded her ignorance in front of him again, he was bound to wonder why she didn't know things Danica Radulesco should know. Which could lead to big trouble.

Dani turned back to the mirror. She had to be darned careful about what she said and how she looked.

Smiling tentatively, she tried to capture the expression in the bridal portrait, but she just couldn't manage it. There wasn't much she could do about her lower lip, which was still swollen from biting it. But anything she *could* do to increase the resemblance would be a good idea.

Taking a blue ribbon from one of the drawers, she pulled her hair back in a reasonable imitation of the style in the painting, then checked her reflection again.

The overall effect wasn't bad. If fact, it was so good that, for the first time, she seriously thought it might be possible to pull this off.

Grabbing her jeans off the floor, she began folding them up to hide in a drawer. A crinkling sound made her check the pocket, and she pulled out a folded sheet of paper.

It took her a moment to realize it was the information sheet about the newly opened library display at Castle Ceistra. She'd picked it up when she'd gone in to see the portrait, but hadn't taken time to read the information then. Glancing at it now, she saw that there were brief notes about each of the major items in the library—the desk, the book collection, and, of course, the portrait.

The large painting is a typical midnineteenth-century bridal portrait. The young woman is Danica Radulesco, only daughter of Count Radulesco, whose family owned Castle Ceistra for more than three hundred years.

Sadly, Danica's husband died while fighting in the revolution of 1848-49. After it was over, she left Transylvania for a time.

When she returned in 1850, a tragic fate awaited her. She was declared a vampire and consequently executed.

Heart pounding, Dani read the words a second time, then a third. No matter how often she reread them, though, they kept saying the same thing.

But Danica Radulesco had *never* returned to Transylvania. The family history was perfectly clear on that. In fact, it was because so many years had passed with no word from a Radulesco, that they'd lost Castle Ceistra forever.

Whoever had written this information sheet, though, must have known *someone* had been killed as a vampire in 1850. Someone who had apparently been taken for Danica Radulesco.

Dani looked into the wardrobe mirror once more. This time, she saw a very frightened woman staring back at her. And little wonder. Here it was, 1850, and here *she* was, in Transylvania, trying to pass as Danica Radulesco, rather than risk being burned at the stake as a lunatic.

But the people who'd set up the library display had relied on local history records. If those records showed that Danica Radulesco was killed as a vampire—here, in 1850—it wasn't too hard to figure out who'd *really* been killed.

It hadn't been the woman in the portrait. It had been the woman in this mirror.

Karsten may have saved her life last night, but she was clearly still in line for a stake through the heart.

Chapter Four

Karsten strode wearily past the tapestries decorating the walls of the great hall and headed into the dining room for breakfast.

His sister was alone, dwarfed by the table that easily sat twenty. She looked eager, as if she'd been waiting to talk to him. Seeing that almost made him groan. He hadn't finished taking care of Ernos's body until dawn, and he wasn't up to facing an interrogation.

When he slumped into the chair opposite Zanna, she poured him coffee, then lifted the top off the silver serving dish. She waited quietly while he slid a couple of dumplings, some venison hash and a few hot biscuits onto his plate. As soon as he took his first bite, she pounced.

"What was going on in the middle of the night?"

"Did none of the servants tell you that Danica is back?"

"Really?" Zanna's face broke into a momentary smile—quickly replaced by a puzzled frown. "It was Danica who screamed?"

Karsten nodded, his mouth full of biscuit. Zanna had been visiting a friend yesterday, and hadn't been home when he'd gone charging down to Biertan Village on Ebony. And, obviously, the servants had kept the gossip about the early evening's happenings to themselves.

That was hardly surprising. None of them would want him to think they even knew what had happened—not after his furious outburst when Ernos admitted drugging Danica and handing her over to the villagers.

"Well?" Zanna pressed. "What made her scream?"

He shrugged, gesturing that she should give him a minute to eat.

There was no point in trying to keep her in the dark about last night. She'd hear all about it in no time, from Danica herself. They'd always confided everything to each other.

And any of the villagers would be happy to fill in the blanks about what had happened while Danica was drugged. Being on the verge of killing a suspected vampire, only to have her whisked out from beneath the stake, would be a major topic of conversation throughout the entire village.

Of course, before he'd left Danica last night, he'd warned her not to say a word to *anyone* about Ernos being murdered. That was one thing the villagers didn't know about, and it had to remain that way for the moment.

So both he and Danica had to be careful of what they told Zanna. She couldn't keep a secret to save her life.

"Danica was in the library and a mouse ran across her foot," he tried, shoveling hash into his mouth so he could leave it at that.

"What was she doing in the library? In the middle of the night?"

"Looking something up."

His sister wrinkled her nose at him, as if to say he was being ridiculous.

"Zanna, I don't know exactly what she was checking. You'll have to ask *her* about that."

"But how did she get back from Walachia? And why didn't anyone tell me she was here when I got home last night? Where is she now?"

Karsten rubbed his jaw. How *had* Danica gotten back from Walachia? In all the excitement, he hadn't thought to ask.

"Karsten," Zanna said impatiently. "I asked you where Danica is now."

"She's in the groundkeeper's cottage. I thought it made sense to put her in there with her things."

"But why hasn't she come to the castle? There's no food in the cottage, so if she's awake she'll be starving. I'll ask Vesna to make some more...oh, that reminds me. Vesna wants to talk to you. I think she must be upset about something. She burned a whole batch of biscuits and she never does anything like that."

Karsten managed to keep from swearing, but just barely.

Not that he hadn't expected this. He'd known Ernos couldn't vanish without his wife noticing. And with his parents in Bucharest, and his brother out hunting for the damned vampire, Karsten was the one the servants would turn to with the morning's problems.

But how was he going to look Vesna in the eye and tell her he had no notion where her husband was?

He shoved back his chair, saying, "I'll go talk to her now. Why don't you run over to the cottage and see if Danica's awake yet?"

"I will in a minute. First, I'm going to go down to the root cellar and get a sack of those bonbons mother has hidden away. You know how Danica loves chocolate."

Zanna dashed off, and Karsten forced himself in the direction of the kitchen. He paused in the doorway, gazing across the immense stone floor at the back of Vesna's stout figure. She was working at the wood stove, stirring a steaming pot of what smelled like rabbit stew.

"You wanted to talk to me, Vesna?"

She turned to him, a worried look on her plump face. "Master Karsten, Ernos is missing. He didn't come to bed at all last night, and I haven't seen him this morning."

"Oh?" Karsten said lamely.

"I thought...you were so angry at him last night..." Vesna paused, staring at the floor, making Karsten feel incredibly guilty.

He knew, as well as she did, that there was only so much a servant could imply about a member of the household's behavior, and she'd gone as far as she could.

"I *was* angry," he said quietly. "But everything turned out all right. I reached Danica in time and she's safe. She's here now, in fact. She'll be wanting breakfast. And I assure you that after I returned from the village ... I assure you that I did Ernos no harm, Vesna."

She looked relieved, which made Karsten feel even more guilty.

"Then what could have happened to him?" she asked.

Karsten almost broke down and told her. It was cruel to be giving her hope.

But if the villagers learned there'd been a vampire murder here last night—after they'd lost their chance to execute Danica—they'd storm the castle. And if being cruel to Vesna would prevent bloodshed, he had little choice.

"I...maybe Ernos had something to attend to," he made himself say. "Away from the castle."

"So late at night? When we all know," Vesna added, lowering her voice to a whisper, "that there's an Un-Dead wandering around out there? And... Master Karsten, what about that scream in the night? When you ordered us all back to our rooms?"

"It was Danica who screamed."

"But why? Did she see something? Something frightening?"

"Vesna, please try not to worry. I'm sure Ernos is ... around here someplace."

She gave an abrupt little nod, and Karsten made a rapid exit, his throat almost as tight as it had been last night—when he'd first shone the lamp on Ernos's bloodless face.

BY THE TIME DANI got her clothes and waist pack hidden, and put the diaries back in the box they'd been packed in, she'd managed to calm down a little.

Just because that information sheet said she'd been killed didn't mean it was going to be so. At least, she didn't think it *had* to be so.

After all, she'd been born in the 1960s. So how could she possibly get killed in the 1850s?

She wished she knew more about the concept of time travel, because she had a horrible suspicion she *could* get killed back here—whether she understood how it all worked or not.

But she wasn't *going* to get killed. There had to be a way of preventing that from happening.

A knock on the cottage door made her jump. Thinking about ending up dead wasn't doing anything good for her nerves.

She hurried across the living room, then paused with her hand on the doorknob, wishing for a peephole.

"Mistress Radulesco?" a male voice called.

Reasoning that someone coming to murder her would try to sneak up on her, not stand waiting at the door, she opened it.

The man outside was in his fifties. A little above average height, with such chalky skin that he looked cadaverous, he had a long nose, brown hair, beady brown eyes and a large mouth that drooped a little to one side.

"Good morning," she offered tentatively, worrying that he was someone who'd expect her to know him.

He didn't smile, and his "good morning" was more a grunt than words. "I come for the dog."

For a second, her mind went blank. "Czar," she finally said, realizing what he was talking about. "He went out...early. He hasn't come back."

"Well he ain't come to the stable for breakfast."

Stable, Dani silently repeated. Was this Letcha, then? The stable master? The same man Karsten had said she'd probably seen walking outside last night? There was no way of telling, when all she'd seen was a cloaked figure.

She realized she'd better say something more, since he was glaring at her as if he suspected she'd garroted the dog during the night.

"I . . . Czar was fine when I let him out."

The man grunted again, then turned on his heel and stomped off toward the pines.

Dani followed him with her eyes. If he *was* Letcha, she hoped he was fonder of animals than he seemed to be of people.

She closed the door, firmly told herself that nothing bad had happened to Czar, then went back to thinking about how she was going to make it through the coming month without being killed as a vampire.

She had a horrible feeling she couldn't manage it alone, but surely Karsten would help her. And she'd learned from the diaries that Zanna Nicholae was her best friend.

At least, she'd been Danica Radulesco's best friend. That was close enough. So she had two people she could trust. Unless . . . well, she just wished she could make that darned legend about the Nicholaes' vampire heritage stop niggling at her brain. So far, she hadn't managed that. Which was ridiculous since she *really* didn't believe that vampires existed.

And even if they did, neither Zanna nor Karsten were Un-Deads. Danica Radulesco surely wouldn't have been best friends with a vampire. And suspecting the worst about Karsten was just plain stupid.

The man had saved her life. Plus, in some of the last year's diary entries, Danica had written about how brave and principled a man he was.

Even though both Count Nicholae and Sigismund had refused to participate in the revolution, Karsten had gone against his father's wishes and secretly worked with the nationalists in some underground organization.

All in all, Karsten Nicholae was *not* likely to be a vampire.

Besides, she had enough to worry about without worrying that every time he came near her he might give her the kiss of death...or was it called the kiss of eternal life?

She shook her head. She didn't have a clue about the finer points of vampirism, and probably the less she tried to figure them out the better.

Besides, regardless of anything else, Karsten wasn't going to be kissing her. She might find him attractive...well, she might find him *darned* attractive, but 1850 Transylvania was definitely neither the time nor the place for her to be thinking about a man. All she wanted from Karsten and Zanna was help in staying alive until she could go back to where she belonged.

Anxiously, she wandered over to the window, then reread the information sheet one more time.

It really gave her the willies—like reading her own obituary. And it left her feeling that, even with two friends, she was going to need an awful lot of luck to survive until the hunter's moon.

Her eye caught a movement outside and her heart began to race. A young woman had just walked through the stand of pines and was hurrying toward the cottage.

Was it Zanna? Or had Karsten sent one of the servants with a message?

Dani quickly refolded the information sheet, looking back outside as she tucked it securely into the pocket of her dress. The fact that she didn't even know whether this woman was her best friend or a servant didn't augur well for her chances of passing as Danica Radulesco for long.

But the woman in the clearing looked to be in her early twenties, the right age for Zanna. She had blond hair, a similar pale shade to Karsten's, and her features were even, like his—just more finely chiseled. She was delicate and pretty and she seemed...well, for all that Dani didn't know about 1850s clothes, she thought the woman was too well dressed to be a servant.

Taking a deep breath, she threw open the door and smiled warmly.

"Oh, Danica!" the woman called. "I'm so glad to see you. I've missed you so much."

Offering up a tiny, hopeful prayer, Dani called, "Oh, Zanna! I've missed you so much, too."

WHEN KARSTEN REACHED the cottage, Danica was just finishing her story about the previous night.

As he stepped inside Zanna turned to him, her blue eyes wide as saucers. "Karsten, what if you'd been too late getting to the village? How could Ernos have done that to her? And then all the others . . . actually ready to *kill* her?"

He shrugged. "The Austrians did a thorough job with their rumors. You know that. And Danica frightened Ernos."

"Dani," Zanna said.

He looked at her blankly.

"She asked me if we'd mind calling her Dani. That's what everyone has been calling her in Walachia, and she's gotten used to it."

"Dani," he repeated. It sounded awfully peculiar on his tongue. And it was hardly worth trying to get accustomed to calling her that when he wanted her gone as soon as possible.

"But how," Zanna asked, "could Ernos have possibly believed our Dani was really a vampire?"

"Well, he assumed *our Dani* had gotten into the castle by turning into a bat. Or mist or something. I'm not sure exactly what he thought. He was practically babbling when he explained about drugging her and everything."

"I just came in through the main entrance," Dani offered quickly. "There didn't seem to be anyone around and . . . I wandered into the library hoping to find someone. . . . I guess I shouldn't have, but I wasn't thinking."

"It's your home, so you had a perfect right just to walk in," Zanna said, passing Dani the bonbons, then taking one herself.

She held the sack out to Karsten but he shook his head. There were only a couple left. If that sack had been full when they'd started, Dani wasn't going to need the breakfast he'd asked Vesna to make.

"But, Dani," Zanna went on, "whatever made you risk coming back so soon? And your mother, did she come, too?"

"No...no, I came alone."

Karsten eyed Danica...*Dani,* he reminded himself, waiting for her to elaborate.

She licked her lips in a nervous little motion that left them moist.

He felt a sudden heat in his groin, then the gradual pressure of the buttons on his breeches beginning to strain a little.

What the devil was going on? Last night he'd ended up deciding it must have been the moonlight that had made him react to her this way.

But now, in the light of day, he found being near her at least as disconcerting. Maybe more so.

Her eyes seemed a warmer, deeper shade of brown. Almost the exact color of those chocolates she and Zanna were just finishing the last two of. And her lips were full and soft and far more lush than he'd recalled.

That, he reminded himself, was because her lower lip was swollen. And he had to be just imagining any other differences.

She bit into the bonbon, then slowly sucked a smudge of melted chocolate off her finger.

Watching, he almost groaned. He forced his eyes from her face, then wished he hadn't. Letting his gaze trail down her body caused his buttons to strain to near the point of popping.

Over the course of the year, her figure had grown far more womanly. That, he was *certain* wasn't his imagination. He'd seen her wearing her blue dress many times, but it had never clung to her curves the way it was clinging this morning.

Casually, he rested one arm on the fireplace mantel, turning sideways enough so that his state wouldn't be noticeable.

"Dani?" Zanna said. "Do tell us all the details. Why ever *did* you come back so soon?"

"I...I was homesick. I wanted to visit with you, Zanna. So badly. And I didn't know...Karsten said he wrote me a letter, but I didn't receive it. So I didn't know there'd be a problem."

"How did you get here?" he asked.

Her face flushed and she looked nervous again. Of course, now that she knew what a serious error she'd made by coming back, it wasn't surprising that she was nervous.

"I...I got a ride. With some friends of our relatives in Walachia. They were coming north and had room in their carriage."

"But where are they? Surely they didn't just leave you standing outside the castle last night?"

"Well, yes. Actually, that's precisely what they did. It was almost dusk when we got here, and they wanted to go a little farther before dark. So they just dropped me off and went on their way. They were in such a rush they even forgot to unload my bag, so it's lucky that you kept my old clothes."

Zanna caught Karsten's eye and raised her eyebrows at him. She was obviously thinking the same thing he was.

What kind of people had Dani traveled with who wouldn't have expected to stay for the night at Castle

Ceistra? Who wouldn't have expected friends of the Radulescos to be greeted with simple hospitality?

He glanced at Dani again, asking, "And when will they be coming back for you?"

"Back. Ahh...in a month. One month. The next full moon, they said. So...it *is* all right if I'm here for a month, isn't it?"

"Of course it is," Zanna said. "I'd be happy if you stayed forever."

"No," Karsten said firmly. "I'm sorry, Dani, but your staying would be far too dangerous."

She glanced from Zanna to him, a pleading look in her dark eyes. "Karsten, I could stay right here in the cottage. It's so nice to be surrounded by all these familiar things. And last night you said I'd be safe here and—"

"I said *safer*. Safer than in the castle itself. Not safe."

"But I'm sure I'd be fine. I've got the gun you lent me. And—"

"Dani, no," Karsten said again. "You just can't stay. It's not a good idea for you to be here for a day, let alone a month. Remember what else I said last night? I said it would be safest for you to go straight back to Walachia, until things have settled down here."

"Well she can't go *straight* back," Zanna said. "She needs some sleep. Look at her. Look at those dark circles around her eyes. She says she stayed up half the night, reading, because she was too upset to sleep."

Karsten started to check Dani's eyes for dark circles, but she was still gazing at him with that pleading expression, so he glanced back at his sister.

"And how's she going to get there?" Zanna demanded. "Until her friends come back for her? The trip takes days. It's much too far to travel on horseback. And Father and Mother have the carriage in Bucharest."

Karsten considered that for a minute, finally saying, "Dani, I'd hire a carriage and take you back myself, but I just can't leave right now. Not until the vampire is found."

"Sigismund and Karsten have been out hunting for it, day and night, since the first body was discovered," Zanna explained. "They think we might have serious trouble with the villagers if it isn't tracked down soon. You know, that silly old legend about the family."

Dani nodded.

"So," Zanna asked, looking at Karsten again, "how *is* she going to get back to Walachia?"

"I guess I'll have to arrange for a carriage *and* driver. Someone from the village."

"From the *village?*" Dani said.

"The *village?*" Zanna echoed.

He cleared his throat uneasily. They had a good point. After last night, how could he trust any of the villagers?

And there really was no possible way *he* could take her. Even if he didn't feel it was crucial to be out hunting for the vampire, there was a chance someone would discover Ernos's body.

If that happened, all hell would break loose. So he couldn't risk being several days' travel away from the castle.

"Karsten?" Dani said.

"Yes?"

"I was just thinking, why couldn't I help you? Help try to find the vampire?"

"Dani!" Zanna exclaimed. "Whatever are you saying? That's a man's job. I'd never even dream of doing such a thing."

"Ahh . . . well, you see, my way of looking at things has changed since I've been living in Walachia. People's attitudes are different there. About what jobs are only for men, I mean."

Karsten gazed at her, his thoughts flashing back to last night. He'd realized then that she'd changed, but hadn't been able to pinpoint exactly how. Was it merely her way of looking at things?

Thinking about last night sent an image of Ernos flickering through Karsten's mind. He saw the servant lying dead, Dani hunkered over him with wet blood on her mouth.

"What?" she said.

"Huh?"

"You're looking at me strangely."

"Oh . . . sorry." He looked away, but the image had jolted his common sense.

Regardless of what he wanted to believe, it was still possible that the villagers were right. Still possible Dani *had* joined the ranks of the Un-Dead, that she *was* responsible for the outbreak of killings.

And her idea about going off vampire hunting with him was so bizarre it made him suspicious. The thought of a woman doing something like that . . . well, even in Walachia, people's attitudes couldn't conceivably be *that* different.

So maybe her suggestion was meant as a ruse. What better way to convince him she couldn't be the vampire than to offer her help with the hunt?

And if she *had* become an Un-Dead, and he ended up alone with her in the mountains . . .

He glanced at Zanna. If he didn't take Dani with him, his sister would no doubt end up alone with her right here in this cottage.

Dani had begun speaking to Zanna again, and he forced his attention back to what she was saying.

"People are much more progressive in Walachia," she was explaining. "They simply don't view everything in terms of men's jobs and women's jobs."

"But Karsten and Sigismund have been staying out in the mountains all night. You'd freeze."

"Oh, Zanna, why would I freeze when they haven't? And," she went on, turning to Karsten, "you have to admit it would be in my own best interest to help. After all, once the *real* vampire is found, the villagers will know it isn't me."

He rubbed his jaw uneasily. The idea of a woman helping hunt for a vampire might be totally ridiculous, but if he couldn't figure out a way of sending her back to Walachia immediately, could he risk letting her out of his sight?

"The idea *does* make sense, doesn't it?" she pressed.

He gazed at her, thinking about the prospect of being alone with her in the mountains. Day *and* night. It gave him the strangest feeling—a combination of uneasiness and desire.

Dani held Karsten's gaze, willing him to go along with her.

In the real world, she'd never dream of suggesting heading off into the wilderness with a man she barely knew. This wasn't the real world, though. At least it wasn't *her* real world. And if she didn't want to end up dead, in the wrong century, she had to do whatever she could to ensure she stayed alive—including trying to help catch the vampire, or whatever it was that was on the loose.

"I won't be a hindrance, Karsten," she tried. "I promise." And she wouldn't be. Having parents who were teachers and nature lovers, she'd spent her childhood summers camping in the mountains of California.

She felt at home in the mountains. And two pairs of eyes were always better than one. And if they could find the real vampire, her odds of surviving until the hunter's moon would soar.

Unless . . . of course . . . the real vampire turned out to be her hunting companion.

She was just about to dismiss that unsettling thought, reminding herself that Karsten was a highly unlikely candidate to win the vampire sweeps, when a shadow fell across the open doorway.

One glance told her this had to be the elder Nicholae brother. He was a slightly older, stockier—and not nearly as attractive—version of Karsten. Not to her mind, at least.

"Sigismund!" Zanna said, running across the room and wrapping her arms around the man's neck. "You're back. And look who's come to visit us."

Sigismund looked. And his stare sent a chill down Dani's spine.

His eyes were blue, like Karsten's.

But Sigismund's eyes were pure ice.

And his gaze was pure hate.

Chapter Five

"Oh, it worries me so when either of them stays out all night like that," Zanna said as Karsten and Sigismund started away from the cottage. "I was awfully concerned about Sigismund. You know, Dani, even the idea of hunting that vampire during the day frightens me. I don't understand how you could possibly consider going along with Karsten."

Dani nodded, trying to pay attention, but all she could think about was the way Sigismund had looked at her. As if breaking her neck would give him the ultimate in pleasure. Or had it been *biting* her neck that he'd been thinking about?

Whichever, his gaze had started her stomach forming knots on top of knots.

Of course, she'd probably only imagined that he'd focused his icy eyes on her throat. And he hadn't given her even the trace of a smile, so she hadn't been able to check for overdeveloped canines.

But if there actually was any truth to the legend about the Nicholae family having a vampire heritage, she'd lay odds she'd just met the member of this generation who'd be walking the earth for eternity.

At least, she realized, that almost put to rest her last lingering doubts that it might be Karsten. There were still a couple of tiny ones left, but the big ones had all just marched firmly into Sigismund's court.

"Oh, Dani," Zanna said, gazing at her intently, "here we've been talking and talking, but I've been saving my most important news for last. And now you look as if you're dying for a nap. You aren't too tired for me to stay a little bit longer, are you?"

"No, no, it's just...Sigismund didn't seem very happy to see me."

"Oh, you know Sigismund." Zanna gave an airy wave of her hand. "He isn't easygoing like Karsten. Besides, he doesn't really know you. He was too old to put up with us the way Karsten and *your* brothers did, remember?"

"Yes, he doesn't really know me. I guess that's all it was."

The diaries hadn't made much mention of Sigismund, and now Dani realized why. She guessed him to be around thirty-five, which would make him about five years older than Karsten and seven years older than her...but roughly *thirteen* years older than Danica Radulesco and Zanna.

It was hard to keep all the details straight, and it didn't help any that she was actually six years older than the woman she was posing as.

At any rate, with such a wide age difference, it was no wonder Sigismund and Danica Radulesco hadn't really known each other.

But not really knowing her, and staring pure hatred at her, were entirely different things.

"I'm sure he'll be friendlier once he's had some sleep," Zanna was saying. "After all, he's been off in the mountains for two straight days."

Dani nodded, wondering if he really *had* been. Or had he been the killer outside the library last night?

She forced her mind to a different subject and asked, "But what's this important news you've been saving for last?"

Zanna clasped her hands in front of her and positively beamed. "I'm betrothed. To a man named Petre Vaidescu. I met him last winter, at a ball in Tirgu-Mures. He's the son of Baron Vaidescu of Brasov."

"Zanna, that's fantastic," Dani said, giving her a hug. "I'm so happy for you. Tell me all about him."

"Oh, he's wonderful, Dani. And he's the *eldest* son."

"Ahh." Historically, in Transylvania, the eldest son inherited everything. Which meant that even if Petre *wasn't* wonderful, he'd be considered a real catch.

"The wedding is to be next spring, Dani. Surely, by then, it'll be safe for you to come back here for good, won't it? I'd feel dreadful if you weren't at my wedding."

Dani simply hugged Zanna again, her thoughts inexplicably drifting to Karsten.

Sigismund was the eldest Nicholae son. And she knew he'd been the one to take over Castle Ceistra—the one who'd been living there when Danica Radulesco's daughter eventually tried to claim it. So what would become of Karsten in the future?

She shook her head, wondering why, with a thousand other things to worry about, that question had popped into her mind.

"GET RID OF HER," Sigismund snapped when they emerged from the stand of pines.

They were the first words he'd uttered since they'd left the cottage, and he accompanied them with the same sidelong glare he'd been using on his younger brother for thirty years.

Ignoring it, Karsten said, "It isn't that easy. There's no way of getting her safely back to Walachia at the moment, so we're stuck with her for a month. Until the people who brought her come back for her."

"No. Find a way, whether it's easy or not. I don't want her here."

Karsten kept his silence as they headed across the cobblestone courtyard to the castle, but he knew why his brother wanted Dani gone.

Her being here, even for a short time, was a reminder to everyone about who the rightful owners of Castle Ceistra were. And from the day his family had moved in, Karsten had gotten the impression that Sigismund hoped Dani and her mother would never return. If they didn't, there'd be no reason for the Nicholaes ever to leave the castle. And eventually, when Sigismund inherited the title of *Count* Nicholae, he'd be lord of the manor.

"Come to the library with me," Sigismund said once they were inside the castle. "There are some things we've got to talk about."

Karsten had been about to suggest a talk himself, so he simply followed along across the entrance hall and down the east wing to the library.

He wished, though, that his brother had suggested someplace else. After last night, it would be hard not to imagine poor Ernos lying on the library floor.

Sigismund closed the door behind them, then turned, saying, "I found another body. Another villager. Old Remus Spoitora, this time."

Karsten sank into the chair behind the desk, feeling ill.

"He couldn't have been killed more than a few hours ago," Sigismund continued. "I came across him on my way home. He was left right outside the castle wall, as if this vampire is taunting us."

"Taunting us," Karsten repeated. If Sigismund thought *that* was taunting them, wait until he heard about the killing right outside that door he'd just closed.

"I performed the ritual on the body, then buried it and the head in separate graves. But if wolves start digging, somebody else is bound to find out that there's been another death."

"You don't think we should just tell people about it? Everyone's going to suspect the worst when they realize Remus is missing."

"Them suspecting is better than them knowing for sure. Every new body only increases the level of hysteria. And now, with four killings—"

"Five."

When Sigismund glanced a question at him, Karsten began with what details he knew about Ernos drugging Dani and didn't stop until he reached the part about finding Ernos dead outside the library.

"Good God," Sigismund muttered when Karsten finally paused. "Danica killed him, then? The villagers were right? She's become a vampire?"

"No. No, it definitely wasn't her," Karsten said, trying to sound as if he was entirely convinced that it wasn't a possibility.

His brother didn't hold with extending the benefit of the doubt. If he started believing that Dani was actually their vampire, he'd have a stake through her heart before she could say "puncture wounds."

"But whoever it was...Sigismund, the vampire killed right inside the castle last night. Between that and leaving Remus's body outside the wall, maybe it isn't that he's trying to taunt us. Maybe he's trying to implicate us—get all of the villagers ruminating about the legend."

His brother swore, pacing across the room.

"And that isn't the only thing this new death has me worrying about, Sigismund. If you say Remus had only been dead for a few hours, then the time between the killings is decreasing. Instead of one a day, now we've had two in less than twelve hours. At this rate, our Un-Dead friend could kill off half the village before we catch him."

Sigismund paced back toward Karsten, a deep frown etched in his forehead. "How many people know about Ernos?"

"Only Dani and me. I mean, obviously he's missing, and Vesna's worried about him. But I hid the body, so nobody should find out what happened until we're ready to tell them."

"Where did you hide it?"

"In the chapel crypt."

"Right in the castle? Why?"

"Because I didn't perform the ritual on it."

"What?" Sigismund yelled.

"For crying out loud, Sigismund, keep your voice down. You know the chances are low that a victim will actually become an Un-Dead. And we're talking about Ernos. Sooner or later, we'll have to tell Vesna and the others. And I'm certainly not telling her I cut off her husband's head and ripped out his heart."

"You'd rather take a chance on his becoming a vampire?" Sigismund snapped.

"That's why I hid the body in the chapel. Even if the worst *did* happen, we'll be safe as long as it's in there. He wouldn't have the power to get out of the coffin as long as it's inside a sanctified place."

"I don't like this," Sigismund muttered. "I don't like a body under the castle roof. We're going to have to move it. And I'll perform the ritual if you can't stomach doing it."

"Fine, we'll move it. But we can't do it right now. Not in broad daylight."

"As soon as possible, then. I don't like a body under the castle roof."

"I heard you the first time. I haven't gone deaf."

Sigismund ignored Karsten's sarcastic tone, saying, "And I don't like that Radulesco woman being here, either."

"I heard you say that, too. But she's the least of our problems."

"Oh? And what if she's not? What if she's our *entire* problem? You don't *know* it wasn't her who killed Ernos. Finding her with the body seems damned incriminating to me. And she could have killed Remus Spoitora just as easily. I don't suppose you had anyone watching the cottage during the night, did you?"

"No, but—"

"Exactly. She could have slipped out and back in with nobody the wiser. And if the villagers find out about either of these new murders...look, this makes it even more critical to get her out of here. Immediately. Take her back to Walachia yourself if you have to, before her being here causes us more trouble."

"Uh-uh. I'm not going all the way to Walachia when there's a vampire killing people right inside the castle. But I'll make sure Danica Radulesco doesn't cause us any more trouble."

"How?"

"I won't let her out of my sight."

DANI AND KARSTEN RODE out of the castle grounds and started down the road that ran beside the stone wall.

Czar and two other wolfhounds raced excitedly ahead of the horses. Obviously, not turning up for Letcha's breakfast hadn't done Czar a bit of harm— even though Dani's heart had dropped when she'd first walked into the stable with Karsten.

From the scowl on Letcha's face, she'd thought something terrible had happened to the dog, and that the stable master considered her responsible. But since Czar was fine, she could only conclude that Letcha didn't like her any more than Sigismund did. The scowl had stayed put the entire time he'd been saddling Gabriel for her.

When she'd mentioned it to Karsten, though, he'd merely shrugged and said, "I'm surprised you don't remember what a strange fellow Letcha is."

She glanced ahead at Czar once more, trying to forget about both Letcha and Sigismund.

The dog was full of energy while she still felt half-asleep. One minute, she'd been in the midst of a nap, trying to catch up on some of the rest she'd missed by reading the diaries all night long; the next, Zanna had been back at the cottage, telling her to hurry and get ready because she was going vampire hunting.

"Karsten?" she said, giving Gabriel a little dig with her heels to get him up beside Ebony.

Karsten glanced over at her.

"I didn't realize we'd be going out quite this soon."

"The situation's getting more urgent. There was a fifth killing, shortly after Ernos was murdered. Sigismund found the body just along here, on his way home this morning."

"Oh." She glanced uneasily over her shoulder, saw nothing alarming, then realized she didn't know what she was looking for.

Somewhere along the line, she'd actually started believing this vampire nonsense could well be for real. And Karsten's news about the fifth body was certainly pushing her thinking further in that direction.

She was supposed to know a lot more about vampires than she did, though. Danica Radulesco would probably have had all the facts at her fingertips. So, to get up to speed, the trick would be to ask questions without making Karsten suspicious.

"Karsten, I've never been on a vampire hunt before," she began. That had to be a safe-enough statement, given Zanna's reaction to the idea of her going on this one. "What *exactly* should I be watching for?"

"Just anything that looks the slightest bit unusual."

"Ahh." That wasn't much help when *everything* looked unusual.

"And you think we might actually find him?" she tried.

"It's possible. Like most vampires, ours probably lies low during the day, when his powers aren't at full strength. But we might be lucky."

"And that gun will be enough if we are?" She skeptically eyed the revolver tucked in Karsten's waistband. It didn't look like much of a match for anything with supernatural powers—even if they weren't at full strength.

"It's loaded with silver bullets."

As far as Karsten was concerned, that apparently explained everything about the gun, so she tried another tack.

"And the dogs will be a help?" She didn't want to come right out and ask whether vampires had a scent. That might be one of the facts she was supposed to know.

Karsten merely shrugged in answer to her question, though, suggesting that he wasn't sure. Vampires, she suspected, weren't an entirely known quantity, even in 1850 Transylvania.

They reached the end of the stone wall and started up a narrow mountain trail. There was no longer room to ride abreast, so Dani dropped back.

Giving Gabriel free rein to follow Ebony, she rode along, watching the way Karsten's body was swaying slightly with his horse's motion, watching the sunlight dance on his hair. Wheat-colored, she decided. That described his hair perfectly.

Astride the big horse, and with that hair, he put her in mind of a cross between a California beach boy and the Marlboro Man—a cross that combined the best of both.

She almost wished she still had more than one or two of those lingering doubts about Karsten's being the vampire. The more she still had, the easier it would be to discount his attractiveness.

Not that she'd been managing that earlier—not entirely, at least. But her suspicions had made it easier. Now she was finding it tough to keep her gaze off him.

Feeling like some sort of cowboy junkie, she eyed the way he was sitting straight and tall in the saddle, looking as if he'd been born to it. She, on the other hand, was feeling about as comfortable as a lobster held over a pot of boiling water.

Ideally, riding in this hot midday sun, she'd be wearing sunglasses, a T-shirt, jeans and a proper cowboy hat. In reality, she was squinting, wearing a ridiculous bonnet and sweltering in a long-sleeved dress that Zanna had identified as a *riding* outfit. All the designation appeared to mean, though, was that there were about a hundred yards of fabric in the skirt, which let her sit astride the horse and still retain the appropriate degree of modesty for 1850.

It could be worse, she told herself. They could be in 1850 England, where she'd have been expected to ride sidesaddle.

After what seemed like forever, Gabriel jolting her bones with each step, they reached a break in the solid face of rock on their right. There was a small but heavenly looking stretch of meadow with a mountain stream gurgling through it.

Karsten reined to a stop. "Hungry yet?" he called, looking back at her.

"Starving." Chocolates for breakfast were divinely decadent, but they hadn't stayed with her the way bacon and eggs would have.

By the time she and her hundred yards of skirt had dismounted, Karsten was digging several cloth-wrapped packages out of his saddlebags.

The dogs nosed around him with great interest for a minute, then suddenly broke into a chorus of howls and took off like the proverbial bats out of hell.

"Rabbit," Karsten explained. "They'll come back in a while. Or else they'll just head home. You do remember this place, don't you?" he asked, smiling at her.

His smile started the strangest little fluttering sensation around her heart.

She nodded, telling herself the sensation was a warning—a reminder to be careful what she said. Hopefully, though, there was nothing specific he expected her to remember about this place.

"How many times did we all picnic here when we were children?" he said.

"Oh . . . so many I couldn't even guess."

Karsten shot her another smile, eliciting another round of flutters.

And, being honest with herself, she had to admit they had nothing to do with warnings. Men she found attractive had always been few and far between, but just looking at Karsten started her pulse racing. If she were back home, alone with him, and he was smiling at her like that . . .

But she *wasn't* back home. And the only thing to do, as far as Karsten's smiles and her flutters were concerned, was ignore them.

Under the circumstances, she simply had to chalk up meeting him to a perfect example of bad timing. It almost made her wish that some ugly little troll of a man had rescued her from the Boar's Head Tavern.

Almost, but not quite, she silently admitted. She let her gaze linger on Karsten for a final second, then forced her attention back to what he'd taken from the saddlebags.

They were obviously going to picnic without a blanket, because he was putting the packages directly on the grass. And, apparently, 1850's picnics didn't include such niceties as plates and cutlery. There were two battered metal cups, though, for whatever was in the wineskin.

Karsten unfolded the cloth wrappings, revealing a loaf of bread, a large chunk of cheese and an equally large slab of meat.

"And Vesna put in some pickled eggs," he said, unwrapping the final parcel. "She remembered how much you like them."

"Yumm...pickled eggs...my favorite." Dani gazed at the unappealing little lumps, trying to look appreciative.

They were hard-boiled eggs that had turned a sickly shade of greenish gray. She couldn't help wondering if that was from the pickling or the passage of time, and just imagining eating one made her stomach feel queasy.

Karsten produced a very large, very sharp-looking knife from his boot. He used it to slice off a chunk of meat, then skewered it on the point and passed it to her.

"Beef?" she asked.

He looked at her strangely, making her remember there weren't many cattle-grazing pastures in the mountains.

"Venison," he said.

Taking a tiny bite, she concentrated on not conjuring up an image of Bambi. The meat was awfully gamy, but the bread and cheese proved delicious.

And the wineskin, thankfully, contained excellent wine. A rich, hearty red that tasted twice as strong as any California burgundy she'd ever had.

She sipped it tentatively, not wanting to think about what the combination of lack of sleep, the sun and alcohol might do to her.

Karsten took another sip of wine and leaned back against a tree trunk, watching Dani through half-closed eyes. She'd taken off her bonnet and her hair had come loose from its ribbon. It looked so soft and silky that he felt an almost uncontrollable urge to touch it. Instead, he looked down at the remains of their lunch.

Dani hadn't eaten much, didn't have anywhere near the appetite he remembered her having.

The thought that vampires had little use for food passed through his mind. Some never even touched it, while others ate occasionally. Even when they did, it was just out of old habit. Only fresh blood was critical to their survival.

He poured a little more of the bloodred wine into Dani's cup, thinking about that fifth killing.

Whether he wanted to or not, he had to admit Sigismund was right. Dani could easily have slipped out of the cottage during the night, could have prowled the countryside for hours, without anyone in the castle knowing.

And she looked as if she hadn't slept much. Of course, she'd told Zanna she'd been up most of the night, reading. But was that what she'd really been doing?

Karsten rested his hand on his chest, feeling the reassuring shape of the crucifix beneath his shirt.

If he encountered the vampire, he'd be ready for it. Even if it turned out that he'd *already* encountered the vampire, he was ready—although the thought of having to kill Dani wasn't one he wanted to dwell on.

"Karsten?"

He glanced at her again.

"Look at the sky," she said anxiously, a sudden clap of thunder punctuating her sentence.

In mere minutes, ominous dark clouds had appeared from nowhere. Driven by a wind as sudden as the clouds themselves, they began rolling over the sun, turning the bright day dull.

Gabriel snickered nervously and skittered a few feet along the stream.

"The cave," Karsten said, sliding his knife back into his boot and pushing himself to his feet.

He quickly grabbed Gabriel's reins in one hand, Ebony's in the other, and started across the clearing.

When he looked back, Dani was frantically gathering up the remains of the picnic.

"Leave it," he called impatiently. He knew how fast the storm would hit.

"We can't just leave such a mess...." Dani caught herself before she called Karsten a litterbug. She dropped the half-eaten food she'd already picked up, keeping only the cups, and hurried after him.

He headed down the stream maybe thirty yards, then stopped and began tying the horses to a tree.

"Go ahead," he ordered. "Get into the cave before the rain starts."

Cave? She might love mountains, but caves weren't on her list of favorite things. Looking uneasily along the mountain face to her left, she tried to locate a cave entrance. All she saw was rock and scrawny bush.

"Go on," Karsten snapped as rain began splashing down.

"I... it's okay. I'll wait for you."

He muttered something while he finished tying Ebony's reins, then dashed toward her.

Not more than six feet from where she was standing, he shoved a few branches aside, fully exposing the opening she'd looked right past.

She gazed at it, telling herself it wasn't really *that* small. And, actually, it wasn't. It was about the size of the doorways in her apartment back home.

But that didn't mean the cave itself would be large. And she *really* didn't like caves—not even big ones.

"Hurry," Karsten ordered.

The rain was pelting down now, rapidly soaking them, but she continued to hesitate.

She'd desperately like to admit to her not-quite-mild problem with claustrophobia. Getting drenched out here in the rain was far preferable to going into that cave.

But she was supposed to be Danica Radulesco, and the woman probably didn't have a claustrophobic bone in her body.

"Come on," Karsten snapped, grabbing her hand.

Dani gritted her teeth and let him drag her into the cave, images of bats fluttering through her mind.

Chapter Six

The moment Karsten pulled her into the cave, Dani knew that her fears had been well-founded. Despite its large opening, the interior was small.

Not far beyond the entrance, the ceiling began to drop sharply. And the light that was coming in quickly dissipated, turning the interior into an eerie twilight zone. It made her extremely anxious.

Karsten hunched his shoulders, continuing to move forward.

"Let's just stay here," she said, jerking on his hand.

"You're still getting wet."

"No, it's fine here. Really." She barely got the words out before the wind swept a sheet of rain in over her.

Karsten grinned, pulling her ahead and down beside him so that they were sitting against the shelter of the back wall.

There, it was much too dim and too small for her liking—not an inch of spare room. At her back and to her left were solid rock. To her right was solid Karsten.

She squirmed around, trying to get even a little comfortable, but all she got was rock sticking into her.

"It seems a lot smaller in here than it did when we were children," Karsten said.

"That's because *we're* so much bigger."

Her logic made him smile, which started that fluttering sensation around her heart once more.

And because he'd turned toward her to speak, his face was so close to hers that his breath was fanning her cheek with its warmth, making her far less aware of her claustrophobia and far more aware of him. The result was a most unsettling mingling of nervousness and excitement.

She reminded herself, one more time, that the best thing she could do was ignore both Karsten's smiles and their effect on her. But it was easier said than done, particularly at such close range.

"It's...cozy," she finally offered, feeling one of them should say *something*.

"And dry," he added, still not taking his eyes from hers.

"Uh-huh. Too bad we didn't make it inside before the rain got us." She rubbed her arms as well as she could in the cramped space, trying to warm them. The rain had made her very wet, very quickly, and the cave was decidedly chilly.

"You know," Karsten said, "you'd be better off if you leaned into me a little more."

Without waiting to hear how she felt about the idea, he eased himself around and cuddled her sideways against his chest, then brushed her hair to one side so that it was away from his face.

"How's that?"

"Fine," she murmured, although *fine* was hardly the word to describe being in his arms.

The cave suddenly didn't seem nearly as frightening. In fact, she'd become barely conscious of being in it. She was finding it extremely difficult to be conscious of anything but Karsten.

His body heat had to be seeping right through her flesh and into her bloodstream, because she was growing hotter by the second.

"Starting to get warmer?" he asked, his breath on the side of her face making her hotter yet.

This time, she merely nodded.

"Good," Karsten said. Then he sat trying to remember if he'd ever before in his life felt the way he was feeling at the moment. He decided there wasn't a chance. If he had, he certainly wouldn't have forgotten about it.

Dani smelled like no other woman he'd ever been close to. He couldn't describe the scent, but it made him think of exotic places and hidden pleasures.

And looking at her…when he'd pushed her hair to one side he'd exposed her neck, and just gazing at it was causing him trouble breathing.

He was also having trouble thinking clearly. Something wasn't quite right about her. For the life of him, though, he couldn't think what it was.

All he *could* think was that by leaning forward, just a little, he'd be able to kiss her. It took every bit of his self-control not to.

He forced himself to remember, yet again, the way she'd looked last night—crouched over Ernos like a she-wolf. Then he thought about old Remus Spoitora, whose body Sigismund had found this morning.

As much as he didn't want to believe there was any possibility...

But dammit, how could he be thinking about kissing Dani when there was even the slightest chance that her kiss might rob him of his eternal soul?

Suddenly, he felt her stiffen in his arms. Then she murmured, "Oh, my Lord," just as he sensed, more than saw, a shadow fall across the light at the entrance.

He looked up and his breath caught with fear.

In the opening stood evil incarnate.

Forcing himself to move slowly, he shifted Dani to the side and shoved himself up.

"Stay back," he whispered, ducking forward to where he could stand straight and face the intruder.

The thing was wearing a long black cape wrapped around it so that not even its eyes were visible, but there was no doubting what it was.

Karsten ripped his shirt open, pulled the silver crucifix from beneath it, and held it out in front of him.

The dark figure uttered a low, guttural sound, much like a beast growling, but made no move to back off.

Resting his other hand on the butt of his revolver, Karsten tried to decide if he should chance using it. His silver bullets would only do the trick if he managed a direct hit to the heart. And that cape made it impossible to tell exactly where the heart was.

If he shot and missed, the creature would likely be on him in a second. And he couldn't hope to overpower a vampire hand to hand, not even during daylight hours.

Clutching the crucifix more firmly, he took a step forward, asking, "What do you want with us?"

"I have come for the woman." The vampire's voice, muffled by the cape, was throaty and altogether chilling.

Karsten tried to ignore the way his heart was pounding so hard the sound was echoing in his ears. "The woman is with me," he said.

"The woman does not belong with you. She belongs with me. She is of my kind."

The vampire extended a black-sheathed arm, reaching his gloved hand out past Karsten to Dani. "Do not be afraid, Danica. I will not harm you. But you are too beautiful for mortal decay. Come with me and I shall grant you the gift of eternal life."

Karsten risked glancing at Dani. She looked frightened half to death.

"She doesn't want your gift," he said, looking back at the dark figure. Brandishing the crucifix before him, he took another step forward.

The vampire still didn't retreat an inch. "She cannot speak for herself?"

"I...I don't want your gift," Dani whispered from behind Karsten.

He took yet another step.

This time, the vampire made an angry hissing noise and shifted back a little.

Karsten drew his gun and aimed it, saying, "Pure silver bullets. I melted the silver myself. And strapped to my horse's saddle is a white thornwood stake. Leave us in peace, vampire. And leave Biertan Village in peace."

"Or?" the vampire snarled.

"Or I shall end your existence."

"I think not." His face still hidden, the vampire turned toward Dani once more. "I shall come to you again, my lovely. In the darkness, I shall come. In the middle of the night. When we can be alone to talk. You do not understand what a wondrous gift I am offering."

His words still hanging, the vampire swirled his cape and vanished from the cave as suddenly as he'd appeared.

Karsten stared after him, resisting the temptation to follow. Vampires were known for their tricks, so leaving Dani alone might be a deadly mistake.

"Dani?" he said, turning.

She was huddled against the back wall, her face ghostly pale. If she'd looked half frightened to death a minute ago, she looked nine-tenths of the way there now.

His heart went out to her, and he knew he'd do whatever it took to protect her from that evil.

"DANI?" KARSTEN REPEATED after a moment.

She tried again to answer, but was still too terrified to make her voice work.

A vampire wanted to grant her the gift of eternal life. And he intended to visit her again—when she was alone, in the middle of the night. That thought was more terrifying than any nightmare imaginable.

Last night she'd coped with finding herself in the wrong century and almost being killed by the villagers.

And today she'd been handling her lack of sleep and the effects of the sun and wine—and even being in this claustrophobic cave. But the prospect of being turned into a vampire was just too much.

This situation she'd landed in...well, she simply couldn't take it. There wasn't a prayer she'd be able to make it through to the hunter's moon, so why was she even trying?

Karsten stepped forward, drew her to her feet, then wordlessly wrapped his arms around her.

In getting at his crucifix he'd torn his shirt open to the waist, and her cheek came to rest against his naked chest. His chest hair softly tickled her skin. For some unfathomable reason, that almost started her crying.

In her world, his comforting strength would have made her feel a thousand times better. In his world, it made her feel even more isolated.

He thought he was holding Danica Radulesco. That's who he was trying to console, not a stranger he had no feelings for at all.

If he knew the truth, if he knew that everything she'd said and done since the moment she'd arrived was a lie...she just couldn't keep it up. Tears began streaming down her face.

"Dani?" Karsten murmured. "It's all right. You're safe." He tucked a finger beneath her chin and tilted her face toward his.

Through her tears, she could see that he was smiling at her—smiling, after they'd just been descended upon by Dracula's double. What on earth did he think there was to smile about?

"Hey," he said. "It's not *all* bad. At least, now, I can stop worrying that *you* might be the vampire."

Something inside her snapped at his words. She jerked away from him.

"The vampire!" she managed to say, fiercely wiping her eyes. "You've still been thinking that *I* could be a vampire?"

His smile vanished. "Ahh...no, I was just teasing."

"No, you weren't!"

"Well...all right, I guess I hadn't *quite* ruled out the possibility. Not quite *entirely*. You haven't exactly—"

"You still thought I could be the vampire! After I decided *hours* ago that it couldn't conceivably be you!"

"You thought it might be *me?* How could you seriously have thought it might be me?"

Karsten's tone was so self-righteously incredulous that she had an insane impulse to bite his neck, just to scare the devil out of him.

She made a concerted effort to calm down, but couldn't. "I can't take this!" she finally cried.

Maybe she hadn't acted on her insane impulse, but she could feel herself losing control—just couldn't stop the words that began pouring out.

"I'm not a quitter, Karsten! Or a loser. Don't you think that. In the real world I breeze through things like tour buses breaking down, medical emergencies and rats in my groups' hotel rooms. And back home I risk..." She paused in frustration, searching for words in Székely.

Not finding them, she simply began substituting English where she needed to. "I risk muggings when I walk and carjackings when I drive. I can cope with things like that, though.

"And with California's water shortages. And with holes in the ozone. But I just can't deal with being in the wrong century. I can't handle a village full of people who want to kill me and a vampire who wants to make me live forever. And I can't cope with the one person I thought might help me get through this actually thinking I'm a godforsaken Un-Dead!"

Gazing up at Karsten, her tears began flowing again. But even with her blurred vision, she could see that she'd been right. The expression on his face said that telling him the truth had made him think she was crazy.

She buried her face in her hands, no longer even caring what happened. If she was meant to die in 1850, so be it. It had to be better than living forever as a vampire.

Karsten cleared his throat, then said, "Ahh...Dani? I didn't exactly understand all you just said. In fact, I hardly understood a word. Could you maybe try to explain it?"

Taking a deep breath, she wiped her eyes once more. There probably wasn't a ghost of a chance she could make him believe her. But she didn't *really* want to die. Or live forever.

DANI STOOD PATIENTLY where Karsten had positioned her when they'd first gotten back to the cottage—directly beside the bridal portrait of Danica Radulesco.

This was the third time he'd asked her to stand there while he compared her to the painting. By now she could have pointed to the place on Danica's neck as accurately as he could.

"Right there," he said, tapping his finger against the painting once more, indicating a spot on the stand-up lace collar of the wedding dress.

"You look so much like her, but the mark on her neck is right there. We used to tease her about it when she was little—tell her that, because it was red, it meant she'd been marked by the devil. And you don't have it."

"No," Dani murmured, still thanking her lucky stars for the missing birthmark. Discovering there was nothing unusual about her neck had gone a long way to convincing Karsten she really wasn't her ancestor.

Convincing him she was actually Danica's great-great-great-great-great-granddaughter, though, had been a little tougher.

"I knew back in the cave that there was something different," he said. "I just couldn't think what. But this whole thing... Dani, I still don't understand how it's possible. People just *can't* travel through time."

"That's what I always thought, too—until I did it. And I don't really understand how it's possible, either. But I *had* heard of the concept before. And I can show you the book of spells in the library. It . . . well, I never in a million years would have imagined the spell would work, but here I am."

"Yes, here you are," he repeated, eyeing her uneasily. "A century and a half earlier than where you belong. I just don't see how that can be."

Giving the portrait a final glance, he wandered back across the living room and sank onto the couch—beside the pile of things she'd dumped out of her waist pack earlier.

Picking up her watch again, he pulled out the *test alarm* button, then grinned, saying, "I swear that noise would wake the dead."

"I bought the loudest one I could find. I'm a really heavy sleeper."

He nodded, then started to examine her driver's license once more. Aside from the watch, the license and her credit cards seemed to fascinate him most.

He'd never seen plastic before, let alone a laminated driver's license. And when he'd asked her to explain what it was for, and she'd gotten onto the subject of—

"Tell me again about *cars*," he demanded, using the English word.

She sat down on the end of the couch and started through the explanation one more time. She was having to use English words quite often—there were some things her grandmother had simply never said in Székely.

Karsten was a fast learner, though. He only needed strange-sounding words repeated once or twice and he had them. As Dani went on about basic car design and performance, he began shaking his head once more.

That made her glad she hadn't told him about airplanes. Hearing that people could fly would *really* freak him out. So, for the moment at least, she'd let him go on thinking she brought her tourists over to Europe by boat.

When she finished speaking, he added, "And cars go faster than the wind," reminding her she'd left out that line this time around.

"Except in gridlock," she told him, then smiled at his puzzled expression while she tried to think of how to put it in his language.

Back in the cave, she wouldn't have thought she'd ever smile again. But, difficult as he found it to accept, Karsten was believing the truth. And that had taken a thousand-pound weight off her shoulders.

She felt as if she really did have a friend here now—and a friend she finally knew couldn't *possibly* be the vampire. After all, Karsten had been right beside her when that vampire had appeared.

"Gridlock is what you get when too many cars are trying to use the same road," she finally explained.

Karsten simply shook his head once more, then glanced at the little pile of her clothes—her sweater, jeans and sneakers. She'd shown him everything she'd thought might possibly help convince him.

"And women actually wear breeches?" he asked for about the tenth time.

She nodded, saying, "Check them out again. I really don't mind your touching them."

Tentatively, he reached for her jeans and ran the zipper up and down a few more times. "Amazing. That really is most amazing."

Her glance flickered to his button fly and she briefly wondered when zippers were invented. Then she quickly looked back up, relieved to find he was paying no attention to her.

He was too fascinated by the way he could bend the rubber sole on her sneaker back and forth.

"So," he finally said, putting down her shoe and looking at her. "You're positive you can't get back to the future until the night of the next full moon?"

"As positive as I *can* be. It's what the book says. But...Karsten, that's a long time to be here. I mean, I was frightened enough about what else the villagers might try before the month was out. But that vampire...you heard what he said. About coming to me again. In the darkness. When I'm alone in the middle of the night."

Just repeating his words made her shudder.

Karsten nodded. "So you can't *be* alone in the middle of the night. It's as simple as that."

"Ahh," she murmured, although it didn't strike her as particularly simple.

Back in the cave, that vampire had appeared in the blink of an eye. And she could hardly go through every night of the next month handcuffed to a guard armed with silver bullets.

"We'll move you into the castle," Karsten said, "and make sure that either Sigismund or I am there every minute."

An image of Karsten's brother flashed into her mind's eye. The expression he was wearing in her imagination was exactly the same as it had been when she'd seen him in reality—his eyes pure ice and his gaze pure hate.

She had a strong suspicion that asking him to watch over her would be like asking the cat to mind the canary.

For all she knew, Sigismund could even be the...she tried once again to banish that legend about the Nicholaes' vampire heritage from her mind, but it still wouldn't be banished.

She'd been right in ruling out Zanna and Karsten, though. That vampire in the cave definitely hadn't been a woman. And it certainly hadn't been Karsten. So, if the legend *were* true, there was only one contender left from this generation.

Neither she nor Karsten had caught even a glimpse of the vampire's face. And his voice, muffled by his cloak, had offered no clue. That meant all they really knew about him was that he was more or less Karsten's size . . . which was also more or less Sigismund's size.

She doubted Karsten would be impressed if she suggested his brother might be an Un-Dead. But the idea of moving into that spooky old castle, where she'd be at Sigismund's tender mercy, was at least as scary as the idea of being alone. Maybe more so.

"Karsten? What you told me last night, that I'd be safer in the cottage than in the castle? Doesn't that still hold true? I mean, there must be a hundred ways someone could get into the castle and there's just one door here."

"I don't know," he said, rubbing his jaw thoughtfully. "One door. A couple of windows. And . . ."

"And?" she pressed.

He shrugged, as if he didn't really want to tell her, but said, "Do you know that a vampire has to be invited before it can go into a building?"

She shook her head.

"Just the first time. After that, they can get inside anytime they like."

"In the form of a bat or mist," she guessed, remembering he'd said something about that.

"Right. So, at one time or another, our vampire must have been invited into Castle Ceistra. That allowed him to get inside last night, when he killed Ernos.''

"But what about the cottage?" Dani held her breath. Maybe, if she didn't step foot out of the cottage for a month, she'd be safe.

"Who knows what's happened over the years," Karsten said. "The cottage has been here as long as the castle itself. But it *might* be secure, and we know the castle isn't.''

"So it would make more sense for me to stay right where I am."

Karsten nodded slowly. "I guess it would. But we can't *rely* on the cottage being safe, so you can't be left alone here—certainly not now that we know the vampire wants you. I'll have to stay here with you."

For a moment, Dani simply stared at him.

"Stay here with me?" she finally said. "You mean *here* with me? In the cottage?"

"Of course. Where else? We just decided there's at least a chance it's safer than the castle, didn't we?"

"Ahh..." She thought hard, sure she had to be missing something.

Maybe, if they were in her modern world, most people wouldn't think much about Karsten moving right into the cottage with her. But surely, in 1850, the idea was scandalous.

And the thought of being under the same roof with him, night after night...

Of course, she *did* trust her self-control—it had never failed her before. But given the way her pulse seemed to start revving up whenever Karsten merely looked at her, she'd be wiser not to—

"What's the problem?" he asked, breaking into her thoughts.

"Well . . . what would people think? About us staying here together," she added at his puzzled look.

"What people?"

"Zanna. And Sigismund. And the servants. And the villagers, if they heard."

Karsten shrugged. "What's for them to think? There's no reason to keep the story of seeing the vampire a secret. And with him threatening you, you need protection. So, obviously, the most sensible plan is for me to stay here with you."

"Oh...of course...obviously." Dani nodded slowly, realizing she was going to have to adjust her way of thinking for the next month. Apparently, the conclusions that people in her world would jump to wouldn't even occur to people in 1850.

"Good, we're agreed then," Karsten said. Now, the only problem with their agreement was going to be keeping his hands off Dani while spending so much time with her. He'd manage it, though. No matter how difficult it proved.

Back in the cave, when he'd been holding her in his arms, he'd wanted never to let her go. Being so close to her had started him thinking all kinds of crazy thoughts. But the only thing to do was forget about them. Completely.

Now that he knew the truth about her, and knew that she'd be leaving, forever, in a month...well, there was something about her that made him feel things he'd never before felt for a woman. *Permanent* kinds of feelings. But there was no possibility of permanence between them.

He dragged his gaze from her. Already he could imagine how he was going to feel when she left. And he'd be the biggest fool in Transylvania if he let anything happen between them that would make her leaving even harder. So he wasn't going to touch her, let alone kiss her and do all the other things he couldn't stop thinking about doing.

"So," he said at last, "when we go to the castle for dinner, we'll get some of my things, and you can tell Zanna about seeing the vampire. That'll ensure all the servants hear the story before the night is done. Then nobody will wonder anything about my being in the cottage."

"But are we going to tell Zanna I'm from the future?"

"No. She really can't keep secrets. It's her worst fault. If she hears one, she always *has* to tell someone. Or else it just slips out. And...look, I think we'd better not tell *anyone*. Not even Sigismund. If word got out that you claim to be from the future, people would decide you're a witch."

"A witch. And would that be better or worse than when they decided I was a vampire?"

"It depends." He grinned. "Would you rather have a stake driven through your heart or be burned alive?"

Chapter Seven

Dani had spent so long telling Karsten about the future that darkness had fallen by the time they left the cottage for the castle. But when it had come to his specific questions about the future of Transylvania, there'd been a lot she couldn't answer.

Her family history had focused on exactly that—her family. She'd only heard bits and pieces about the country, itself, as they'd related to her ancestors' lives.

She'd told him all she could, though, and now she was wishing they hadn't talked for quite so long.

The rain that had driven them into the cave earlier had stopped hours ago. But the clouds remained, and the night was so dark and muggy that the walk to the castle was making her uneasy.

The only light came from the coal-oil lantern Karsten was carrying, and it didn't offer enough illumination to make Dani less nervous. She resisted the urge to reach for his hand, and shoved her own hands into the pockets of her dress.

"1867," he said, referring back to what they'd been last talking about in the cottage. "That's a whole seventeen years from now. You're *sure* the occupation doesn't end until 1867?''

"Yes. That's one of the few dates I *do* remember, because it wasn't until the Austrians finally left—until Transylvania was recognized as a country again—that Danica's daughter came and tried to claim Castle Ceistra. And that was in 1867.''

"And Danica was already dead. She dies so young,'' Karsten said, shaking his head.

"My grandmother says that she died of a broken heart—only lived as long as she did because she had her daughter to care for.''

"And damned Sigismund wouldn't give the castle back,'' Karsten muttered.

He glanced at Dani when she didn't reply, saying, "That's why he wasn't exactly pleasant to you this morning, you know. He's afraid you'll decide to stay here and reclaim the castle.''

"Ahh,'' she murmured. That explained one little mystery. Now, if she could just find out why Letcha disliked her, she'd be batting a thousand.

"But try to remember *anything* else your grandmother might have said,'' Karsten was going on. "When the Austrians were eventually convinced to end the occupation...you're sure you don't remember *any* names? She *must* have at least talked about the leader who finally secured our independence.''

"I don't think so, Karsten. She really just told me about the Radulescos. The only reason I recognized Sigismund's name was because of the thing with the castle.''

As she finished speaking, Dani heard the sound of muffled footsteps moving ahead of them through the pines. Her heart leapt to her throat.

Was it the vampire? Hoping to find her alone? In the darkness? Maybe he'd decided not to bother waiting for the middle of the night.

"Who's there?" Karsten demanded, quickly drawing his revolver.

"It's me. Sigismund."

Hearing that didn't exactly flood Dani with relief. It also didn't, in her mind at least, answer the question, Was it the vampire?

She hadn't said a word about her suspicions to Karsten, but she hadn't been able to shake them.

Karsten, though, obviously had no concerns. He was already sticking his gun back into his belt when Sigismund materialized before them.

Even with only the dim light of the lantern, she caught the unfriendly look he shot her way before focusing his attention on his brother. At least now, though, she knew *why* he didn't like her.

"Karsten, I want you to help me with that thing we talked about moving," he said, turning and starting back toward the castle with them.

"Sure. But later, huh?"

"No, now. I want to get it out of the castle. And this is a good time, before these clouds blow over."

"Look, that can wait. Right now Dani and I want to have dinner and—"

"There *is* no dinner. Vesna's disappeared."

An icy chill crept up Dani's spine. Had the vampire killed Ernos's wife, as well?

"What do you mean, disappeared?" Karsten said, sounding so uneasy that Dani knew he was wondering the same thing.

"I mean, she's nowhere around. We're stuck with nothing but a cold collation for dinner, so you may as well help me before you eat."

"Yeah...yeah, all right," Karsten said reluctantly. He didn't relish the prospect of moving Ernos's body from the chapel. And he *sure* didn't relish the idea of Sigismund desecrating it with the ritual.

"Sigismund and I won't be long," he told Dani as they neared the castle entrance. "Why don't you go talk to Zanna for a while? Fill her in on our adventure this afternoon."

"Adventure?" Sigismund said.

"Yeah, I'll tell you about it while we work."

Zanna was in the entrance foyer, obviously waiting for them, and happily whisked Dani off.

Karsten exchanged his lantern for a lamp. Then, as he and Sigismund started for the chapel, he began the story of the vampire appearing in the cave.

"I told you she'd cause us more trouble if she stayed," Sigismund snapped when Karsten finished.

"But you know," he added after a few moments, "maybe her staying isn't really such a bad idea. It means that if the vampire wants her, he'll have to come here. That would make things easier than us riding all over the countryside trying to find him."

Karsten could feel his jaw clenching at the idea of Dani being vampire bait. But he knew Sigismund was right. If the vampire wanted her, and she was at Castle Ceistra, her presence would lure him here.

"Sigismund, I'm going to start staying in the cottage at night. After what happened this afternoon, someone has to be with Dani in case the creature *does* come. But... I'm going to need some help from you on that."

Sigismund gave him a disapproving glare. "How many times do I have to tell you I want you to stop what you're doing? And you know Father feels the same way."

"It's not something I *can* stop," Karsten said, hoping Sigismund would drop the issue. They'd been through it too many times already.

They reached the chapel and Karsten unhappily led the way down the side wall that comprised the crypt. Generations of Radulescos had been buried in this chapel, but each vault had room for several full-size coffins, and he'd easily found an empty, unsealed compartment.

"This one," he said, pointing to a door on the second level, about waist high from the floor.

With the creak of metal on metal echoing through the chapel, he swung open the vault's door. Stepping back, he shone the light into the opening. Since it was Sigismund who was insisting on the ritual, he could take charge from here.

Sigismund maneuvered the coffin into position to pull it out easily, then said, "All right. Give me a hand and let's get it all the way out."

Karsten put the lamp down on the stone floor and got a grip on one end of the casket. The moment they slid it fully out, he knew something was wrong.

"It's too light," both men said at once.

They lowered it to the floor and Karsten glanced uneasily at Sigismund.

Then they lifted the lid.

The coffin was empty.

WITH A JOB that meant being in a different city almost every day, Dani had learned to sleep soundly in unfamiliar places. She seldom woke during the night, no matter where she was. Even, it had turned out, if she was in the wrong century. But, as usual, the first fingers of dawn that snuck in through the bedroom window woke her.

Czar, who always seemed to know the moment she was awake, scrambled to his feet and tentatively poked his wet nose into her face. She scratched behind his ear. They'd developed a little morning routine over the past couple of weeks.

More than a couple of weeks now, she mentally corrected herself. It was getting near three. And here she still was, neither dead, courtesy of the villagers, nor doomed to live for eternity, courtesy of the vampire.

In fact, since that incident in the cave, she and Karsten hadn't encountered any excitement at all.

Oh, there'd been the fright Vesna had given everyone about that same time. But her disappearance had turned out to be nothing. She'd simply gone to visit someone in the village, then hadn't returned until morning because of the stormy weather.

Aside from that, life at Castle Ceistra had been going along normally.

Dani grabbed her robe from the bedside chair and got up to let Czar out, wishing her emotional life had been going along normally as well. It was further from normal, though, than she could ever have imagined possible.

Quietly, she opened and closed the cottage door, carefully locking it once more. Then she glanced across at the couch to make sure she hadn't disturbed Karsten.

He seemed tired much of the time, and she suspected it was because he stayed awake half the night while she was asleep, watching over her like a guardian angel. He even slept in his clothes, so he'd be ready if anything happened.

Her eyes lingered on him. His long pale hair, loose around his face, softened the chiseled masculinity of his features. Still, he positively exuded sex appeal.

So much so, that at first she'd managed to dismiss her feelings for him as simple physical attraction. But every hour she'd spent with him had made it harder and harder to deny there was far more than sexual magnetism between them.

They were so easy together it was incredible. Their daily rides were ostensibly to look for the vampire, but mostly they just enjoyed the mountains. And each other's company.

Then, after dinner at night, they usually played cards in the cottage with Zanna. And once she went back to the castle, Karsten and Dani would sit for hours in front of the fire, telling each other about 1850 and about the future, unable to say good-night, just like *any* two lovers.

But they weren't lovers, and her constant ache of unquenched desire didn't let her forget that for a second.

She doubted Karsten forgot it often, either. Even though he hadn't said anything, she had absolutely no doubt how he felt about her. She could see love in his eyes every time he looked at her. But both his common sense and his willpower were clearly as strong as hers.

He had to have realized, just as she had, that admitting how they felt or, worse yet, succumbing to their desires, would just make things harder in the long run.

The moment the moon waxed full she'd be going. Barely more than a week now, and she'd never see Karsten again. That was going to be bad enough, the way things stood, but it would be even worse if they didn't keep up the pretense of feeling nothing more than friendship.

So no matter how desperately she wanted to touch Karsten, to kiss him, to make love with him, she wasn't going to. Even though all he had to do was glance her way to make her feel as if she'd just been struck by lightning.

She started back to the bedroom; halfway there he stopped her with a "Good morning."

"Good morning," she replied, looking over at him again.

He gave her a sleepy smile that almost melted her on the spot.

"You want to go riding after breakfast?" he asked.

"Sure." Once she made it through Letcha's ritual of shooting black looks her way while he readied the horses, she loved their rides.

She was just about to say something else when there was a rapid knocking on the door, quickly followed by Zanna's voice.

"Karsten? Karsten, are you awake? There's trouble."

Dani hurried back across to the door and unlocked it while Karsten began yanking on his boots.

Zanna hadn't even taken time to pin her hair up, and the hard way she was breathing said she'd run the entire distance from the castle.

"What's wrong?" Karsten demanded.

"It's men from the village. A whole group of them are here. From what little I caught, I think that time Vesna was gone all night she went to see the—"

Zanna completed her sentence with a word Dani had trouble mentally translating, and it took a second for her to realize who Vesna had gone to see. The term didn't have a precise English translation. *Village leader,* maybe? Or *mayor?* Yes, *mayor* was probably as close as she'd get.

"And Vesna told him something," Zanna was continuing. "I'm not sure what, but everyone seems to believe something awful happened to Ernos. And now I think she's left us. There's no sign of her this morning and no fire in the stove.

"And...oh, Karsten, do hurry. Sigismund is in a temper about the men coming here, and he's bound to make them even angrier."

"Wait for me," Dani said, dashing for the bedroom. "I can be dressed in two seconds."

"No," Karsten snapped. "You stay in the cottage. Both of you. Do you have a gun, Zanna?"

She shook her head, clearly frightened.

He grabbed a rifle from the gun rack and handed it to her, then stuck his revolver in his belt.

"Make sure *your* gun is loaded," he told Dani. "Lock the door when I leave, and don't unlock it to anyone except Sigismund or me."

"Oh, dear," Zanna murmured as he headed out.

While she hurried to lock the door, Karsten's final phrase echoed in Dani's mind. "*Sigismund* or me."

He was certain she'd be safe with Sigismund, but her worries about him still hadn't gone away. In the past couple of weeks, there'd been three more vampire killings, and she couldn't help wondering...

She forced her thoughts back to the moment, asking Zanna, "You don't know *exactly* what Vesna told the mayor?"

"Not exactly. But I *do* think it was about something happening to Ernos. And maybe that we didn't tell Vesna about whatever it was. Oh, Dani, that's so silly, isn't it?"

She nodded, hoping her expression wasn't giving anything away. Only she, Karsten and Sigismund knew the vampire had gotten Ernos.

"You know, things aren't the way they were when your family lived in Castle Ceistra," Zanna offered.

Dani stood waiting for her to elaborate.

"The Radulescos lived here for so many generations that the villagers never questioned anything you did. Your father was lord and master, just like your grandfather before him. And whatever any Count Radulesco said was the law.

"But our family...Dani, the villagers don't think we belong in Castle Ceistra. They resent us living in the Radulesco castle. And Romulus Teodescu is especially envious."

Romulus Teodescu. That name rang a faint bell. Danica Radulesco had mentioned the man in her diaries . . . but in what context?

"Of course, that's partly because he hoped to live here himself," Zanna continued. "But you weren't having any of that."

"No, I wasn't," Dani murmured, still trying to remember what she'd read. Was Romulus Teodescu the villager who'd once wanted to marry Danica? Yes, that sounded right.

And Count Radulesco had been appalled at the man's nerve in asking for her hand—even though Romulus Teodescu *had* inherited the Boar's Head Tavern, which made him the richest man in Biertan Village.

Danica, Dani recalled, had told her father that Romulus was only interested in Castle Ceistra and that she'd rather marry a baboon.

"Now that your family is gone," Zanna was going on, "Romulus thinks *he* should be the man everyone looks to. Not my father."

"Yes, Romulus Teodescu *would* think that way," Dani said, although she wasn't quite sure why he would. Maybe because of his relative wealth?

"I think it's because he was chosen mayor when he was so young," Zanna said, explaining the *why*. "He might only be Sigismund's age, but he thinks he knows everything."

Dani simply nodded, tucking the new facts away for future reference.

Then her thoughts returned to the men who'd just arrived at the castle. Her curiosity about why they'd come was growing stronger by the minute.

After her first encounter with the villagers, she wasn't exactly eager for a second. But she was dying to know what was happening.

What if Zanna was wrong, and the men hadn't come entirely because of Ernos? What if they had something on their minds that involved her?

"Maybe... Zanna, do you think we should go and see why the villagers are here?"

"No. I think you should get dressed. Then we should simply wait, the way Karsten told us to. With our guns."

"All right." Dani absently pushed her tangled hair back from her face and turned toward the bedroom.

"Dani?"

She glanced at Zanna and her heart skipped a beat. Zanna was staring at her neck, at the precise spot where Danica Radulesco's birthmark would have been.

Dani's hand flew to her throat, but she knew it was too late. She'd been so careful about keeping her neck covered, but there were no collars on her nightgown or robe.

"You aren't Danica," Zanna whispered, her eyes wide. "Who are you? Oh, my... are you the vampire? Deceiving us by posing as my friend?"

"No! No, I'm not. Really." Dani started toward Zanna, desperately trying to think of a cover story that would sound plausible.

Quick as a flash, Zanna leveled the rifle she was

holding. "Stay back! You *are* the vampire. The villagers were right. And I'm going to go and tell them so!"

KARSTEN REACHED the edge of the pines and stopped to assess the situation. Just as Zanna had reported, there was a whole contingent of men from the village. Close to twenty, he guessed. And she'd thought their visit had something to do with Ernos.

What, though?

He hadn't been able to stop worrying about Ernos's body vanishing, but he'd kept his worries to himself—hadn't even said anything to Dani about its disappearance.

She'd have asked how that could happen, and the most likely explanation was that Ernos had joined the ranks of the Un-Dead. And telling Dani that would only have terrified her.

But *had* Ernos become a vampire? Had he appeared in the village as an Un-Dead? Is that what had these men looking so upset?

Damn! So much for his ever thinking it would be safe to put the body in the chapel. So much for the story that it took three days for a vampire's victim to resurrect as a vampire himself. That body had disappeared within twenty-four hours. Lately, Karsten had been learning that vampire lore was full of misinformation.

Slowly, he scanned the crowd. To a man, they were wearing silver crucifixes. He doubted that was a good sign. It looked as if they'd come expecting to beard a Nicholae vampire in his castle.

Except for the mayor, they were all hanging back in a group. But Romulus Teodescu was standing directly outside the main entrance, toe-to-toe with Sigismund. It was a toss-up as to which of them looked angrier.

Rapidly, Karsten strode across the courtyard to his brother's side and asked what was going on.

"They've come here with some ridiculous story about Ernos," Sigismund snapped.

"It's not a ridiculous story," Romulus snapped back. "It's true.

"Ernos and his wife sought refuge in my house almost three weeks ago," he went on, turning to Karsten. "But I made Vesna come back to the castle until...I made her come back so you two wouldn't suspect that we knew about what had happened here."

"Vesna and Ernos," Karsten said, hoping he sounded a whole lot calmer than he felt. "And what were they seeking refuge from?"

"From the vampire, of course. Since you both want to pretend you don't know, I'll tell you exactly what happened. The vampire almost killed Ernos. Inside Castle Ceistra. Which means one of you Nicholaes is the vampire."

Romulus was speaking loudly, and angry murmurs erupted among the villagers at his accusation.

"Just a minute," Karsten said, holding up a hand for silence. "No Nicholae is a vampire. Now, I don't know what you think happened here, but—"

"Perhaps I can make things clear," a man said in a reasonable tone. He moved out of the crowd and started toward them.

Karsten's glance flickered from the man to the animal he had on a lead. Big and gray, with yellow eyes, it looked more like a wolf than a dog. But it was behaving like a dog, walking docilely alongside its master.

Focusing on the man again, Karsten decided he'd never seen him before. He was maybe fifteen years older than the mayor, probably about fifty. And whereas Romulus was tall and fit, this man was very short and slight, with a beak of a nose and thinning gray hair. Despite his unprepossessing appearance, though, there was an air about him that said he was someone to be reckoned with.

"And you are...?" Sigismund demanded before Karsten could ask.

The man removed his cap with a little flourish. "I am Ion Dobrin, from the city of Timisoara."

"That's a long way from Biertan Village," Karsten said.

"Yes, it took me some time to get here. But I'm used to traveling. My work carries me to all parts of Transylvania."

"And your work is?"

"I am a vampire hunter." As he said the words, Ion stared directly into Karsten's eyes.

Karsten held his gaze steady until the man finally spoke again.

"As your good mayor has told you," he said, his gaze now taking in both Nicholae brothers, "Ernos was attacked by a vampire, inside the castle. Fortunately, he was only incapacitated. Unfortunately, the creature came up behind him and he didn't get a clear look at it."

"Only incapacitated?" Karsten said uncertainly. "You're saying the vampire attacked Ernos but didn't kill him?" He'd been positive Ernos was dead that first night.

"Precisely. The man's blood was drained but he wasn't killed. That happens. And, as frequently follows when it does, the victim fell into a trancelike state.

"This is where the story becomes peculiar," Ion continued. "When Ernos eventually regained consciousness, sometime the following day, he found himself inside a coffin, in the crypt of the castle chapel. He managed to escape from that imprisonment, went to his wife, and she brought him to the village for doctoring. And refuge."

"Then what you're telling us," Sigismund said, "is that after the vampire drained Ernos's blood, he put him in the crypt?"

Ion shook his head. "*Someone* put him in that coffin, but it would not have been the vampire. No UnDead would ever set foot in a chapel."

"So?" Karsten pressed. "Exactly what *are* you saying?"

"I'm saying that the trancelike state is often mistaken for death by the unknowing, and that must be what happened here. And I'm saying that someone in the castle tried to cover up the vampire's attack by disposing of the body. Now, this is a very strange happening, is it not? That *anyone* should try to hide a vampire's evil deed?"

"Very strange," Karsten said slowly, thinking rapidly.

So Ernos hadn't become an Un-Dead, after all. A professional vampire hunter certainly wouldn't be mistaken about a victim's state.

Romulus Teodescu cleared his throat. "I have hired Ion Dobrin to determine who the vampire among us is," he said, glancing from Karsten to Sigismund, as if certain there were only two possibilities.

"*We* will determine who the vampire is," Sigismund told him. "It is the duty of the lord and master of Castle Ceistra to protect the villagers from evils. And, in my father's absence, my brother and I have taken on the responsibility. We need no outsider's help."

"No?" Romulus said. "Well, I think you do. That vampire has been killing our friends for weeks now, and I say we need an expert."

"Perhaps," Ion Dobrin suggested, "the three of us could work together." His glance took in both Karsten and Sigismund once more. "With an attack happening inside Castle Ceistra, and then the strange attempt to conceal the body, I know you will want to cooperate with me."

"And it would be best," Romulus quickly put in, "if Ion stayed right here in the castle with you until the vampire's identity is known."

"Yes. That's an excellent suggestion," Ion agreed.

Sigismund muttered something under his breath.

Karsten shot him a sidelong glance, warning him to keep his temper in check, then looked back at Ion. "Let me speak to my brother in private for a minute."

"Certainly," Ion said. He took Romulus firmly by the arm and moved him away a few yards.

"I don't think we've got any choice but to go along with this," Karsten said once they were beyond hearing range.

"Are you out of your mind? That little snake in the grass wants to stay in the castle so he can spy on us. He thinks one of us is the vampire. Look at them," Sigismund added, gesturing toward the villagers. "They all do."

"Of course they do. They probably haven't been talking about much else but that cursed family legend since the killings began. And with them knowing Ernos was attacked right inside the castle..."

"Well, I don't care what they think," Sigismund snapped. "I'm not playing host to any vampire hunter. The only reason Romulus brought him from Timisoara is so he can point a finger at one of us."

"Right. I'm sure that's exactly it. But what's going to happen if we refuse to cooperate? It'll look as if we don't really want the vampire found, and that would just make the villagers *more* convinced that it's one of us. Hell, they'd probably try to torch the castle."

Sigismund frowned, hard and long, but eventually nodded. "I guess you're right. I guess we have no choice. But a vampire hunter spying on us in our own castle? I sure as hell don't like the idea."

Chapter Eight

The last of the villagers trailed out of the castle grounds, leaving Ion Dobrin and his dog with the reluctant Nicholaes.

Ion stood, hands on his scrawny hips, slowly surveying the courtyard. Then he gestured toward the stand of pines, saying, "Is that the woman people suspected of being the vampire?"

"No," Karsten said, looking over and spotting Zanna. "That's our sister."

He tossed her an annoyed glare, even though she was too far away to catch it. He'd told her to stay in the cottage. If he were tougher on her, the way Sigismund was, she'd listen to him more often.

"I would very much like to meet her," Ion said.

Sigismund glanced sharply at Karsten.

He nodded to say they'd both had the same thought. The less chance Ion had to talk to Zanna before she knew what was going on, the better. Even forewarned, she couldn't be relied on to be entirely circumspect.

"First, we'll get you settled in a room, Ion," Sigismund said. "Letcha?" he hollered.

Karsten hadn't noticed the stable master lurking, but Sigismund obviously had.

As Letcha hurried toward them, Ion's big dog began to growl at him, hackles raised. Ion reached down and grabbed the dog's collar. Absently, Karsten thought how unusual its reaction was. Animals generally took to Letcha instantly.

"Letcha will take your dog," Sigismund was saying. "We keep several of our own in the stable."

"Oh, no," Ion said firmly. "Lupus stays with me. We're a team. He helps with my hunts."

Lupus, Karsten repeated to himself. Latin for *wolf.* Maybe his initial thought about the beast's species had been right.

Sigismund gave the vampire hunter a black look and turned to Letcha. "Just bring Mr. Dobrin's bag along for him, then. His dog won't be staying in the stable."

Letcha hesitated, staying out of the dog's lunging range until Sigismund grabbed Ion by the arm and began dragging both man and wolf-dog off toward the castle. Letcha picked up Ion's bag and followed along at a safe distance.

Zanna was already hurrying across the courtyard, practically dancing with excitement. "Karsten," she began before she'd even reached him, "why didn't you tell me about Dani?"

"What about her?"

"You *know* what about her! About her not really being Danica. About her being from the future! Oh, how could you not have told me? Karsten, she showed me all her things. Aren't they wonderful? Isn't it just too thrilling?"

"Yes. Thrilling," he agreed, trying to smile. Why the hell had Dani said anything? He'd told her not to, not under any circumstances. And he'd particularly warned her not to say anything to Zanna.

"Oh, I didn't think to ask her," Zanna said, "but does Sigismund know?"

"Not yet," Karsten admitted, silently cursing. Now he had to tell Sigismund.

If he didn't, Zanna would for sure, and their brother would have a hard enough time believing the truth from him, let alone from her.

If Sigismund didn't believe Dani's story, though, he'd be every bit as quick as the villagers to brand her a witch.

"Aren't you going to tell me what all those men wanted?" Zanna asked.

Karsten recounted the visit, making it sound as if this had been the first he'd heard about anything happening to Ernos.

He was careful not to add any details that the villagers didn't already know. The last thing he wanted was Zanna telling people *he'd* been the one who'd hidden Ernos in the crypt.

Even without added details, her eyes grew wider with each word he spoke.

"So the vampire came right inside the castle, then?" she whispered when he was done.

"Yes. Which means that you've got to be very careful, Zanna. Especially at night. You shouldn't—"

Sigismund, who'd reappeared from inside, waved his hand to cut Karsten off. "Go away, Zanna," he snapped. "I've got to talk to Karsten alone."

She moved off a few feet, clearly not wanting to move an inch, then stood pretending she wasn't trying to overhear.

"Did you warn her about talking to our guest?" Sigismund asked.

"I told her who he was and what he claims to be doing here, but I didn't warn her off him yet. Why don't you do that? You're more effective at putting fear into her."

Sigismund nodded, then glanced over at Zanna. "Come back here."

She started over to them again, glancing curiously at Karsten. "You didn't say two words. You didn't tell him about Dani. Aren't you going to?"

"What about Dani?" Sigismund demanded.

Karsten ignored him, focusing on Zanna. "I'll tell him in a minute. But I don't want you saying anything more about it, understand? Didn't Dani explain to you how important it is not to tell anybody?"

"Yes. She told me a hundred times. But I'm certain she didn't mean Sigismund."

"Well, make darned sure you don't say anything in front of anyone else. It's *extremely* important. You have to swear not to say a word."

"I already swore. To Dani. Karsten, I know things sometimes come out when I don't mean them to, but I'll be ever so careful about this."

"What the hell are you two talking about?" Sigismund snapped.

"You were going to tell Zanna about Ion Dobrin," Karsten reminded him.

"Yes. Zanna, that vampire hunter is going to be staying in the castle for a while, but I don't want you talking to him. Understand?"

"Not even hello?"

"No conversations, I mean. And if he asks you any questions, avoid answering them."

When Zanna nodded, Karsten said, "Sigismund, come to the cottage with me for a minute."

"No, I've got matters to deal with. And I don't want that damned vampire hunter poking around the castle without one of us watching him."

"Sigismund, just come with me. This really *is* important. Dani has some things you'd better have a look at."

KARSTEN CLOSED the cottage door behind Sigismund, then turned to Dani.

She gave him a nervous little smile. "He believed it, didn't he? In the end?"

"Yes, he believed it," Karsten told her wearily. But the more people who knew she claimed to be from the future, the greater her risk. Already, he could practically see the villagers trying to burn her at the stake. And if anything happened to Dani...

Looking away from her, he stood gazing out the window, trying to convince himself that he didn't really care. But he couldn't fool himself.

In the short time she'd been here, he'd come to care for her more than he'd ever cared for anyone. He hadn't meant it to happen. In fact, he'd fought like crazy against it happening. But it had.

From that moment in the cave, when he'd held her in his arms, he'd been able to think of almost nothing except holding her again. He'd resisted the desire, though, even when it had taken more willpower than he'd known he had.

Over the past weeks, he'd reminded himself a hundred times a day that she'd soon be leaving him. And he was *helping* her. Keeping her safe so that she could make her way back home.

Every time he thought about that it stuck in his craw. He wanted her to stay forever and he was helping her go. But what else could he do?

He'd help her and she'd leave—assuming she made it through to the hunter's moon alive. Which, he added anxiously to himself, had just gotten a whole lot more difficult to count on.

How could she have been so stupid as to confide in his sister? After he'd specifically warned her not to? She was no better than Zanna, herself, when it came to keeping a secret.

"Karsten?" Dani said.

He turned to her again.

"You seem awfully worried. What's the matter?"

She didn't even know? He raised his hands in frustration, saying, "Dani, what could possibly have made you say anything to Zanna?"

"I...I had no choice. She saw that I didn't have the birthmark, and it made her think I was a vampire, impersonating Danica. She was going to go right then and there to tell that whole group of men. I had to say something to stop her."

"Well couldn't you have said something else? *Anything* else? I *told* you Zanna can't keep secrets. I told you that over and over again."

For a moment, Dani simply looked at him. Then her lower lip began to tremble.

"I tried to think of something else," she said, her voice shaky. "But it's hard to think when someone's pointing a rifle at you. And she..."

A single tear trickled down Dani's cheek.

Karsten suddenly felt like the worst ogre in the world. "Dani...it's okay. I'm sorry. I didn't realize you had no choice. I'm just worried about what might happen."

A tear escaped down her other cheek and she brushed it fiercely away. "Karsten, don't you think I'm worried, too? I didn't want to tell her, but I'm certain this is one secret she'll keep. She promised me she would and I..."

Dani began staring at the floor, and he knew her tears had won out. Now he felt like the worst ogre in the entire *universe*.

"Dani?" he murmured.

She made a tiny animal noise in her throat and wiped her eyes.

He stood eyeing her for another second. Then, even though his brain was ordering him not to move a muscle, his feet were stepping forward and his arms were reaching for her. He wrapped them around her and pulled her to him.

"Oh, Karsten," she whispered, looking up at him, her eyes luminous. "Oh, Karsten, I'm sorry I'm causing you so much trouble."

"Shhh," he murmured, hesitantly brushing her hair back from her face.

Her body, incredibly soft against his, was making him so hard he ached. Touching her hair was like touching silk, and it smelled like the first wildflowers of spring. And the way she was looking at him, her lower lip still trembling...

Desire swept him—with all the suddenness and intensity of the storm that had rolled in over their picnic and driven them into the cave that first day he'd held her.

Resistance was impossible. He leaned down and kissed her.

Her lips were as soft and warm as the rest of her, velvet against his. He tried to be gentle, but he wanted to devour her with the passion that was devouring him.

Then she slowly moved the tip of her tongue across his mouth, slipping it between his lips a little, and he almost exploded.

"My God," he whispered, drawing back and gazing down at her in amazement.

Her face turned the most delectable shade of pink he'd ever seen.

"I...ahh, Karsten, I think maybe I just gave you the wrong impression and I didn't mean to. I'm not...oh, Lord, I don't even know what the word is in Székely. But I'm not...I mean, I don't routinely kiss men. Don't kiss them at all, let alone that way. I'm a *good* woman. Like Zanna. It's just that in my world...well, things are a lot different between men and women than they are in 1850."

"A lot different how?" he pressed when she didn't go on.

"Well...if a woman...ahh...*responds* to a man she's attracted to, he doesn't think badly of her for it."

"No, no," he said quickly. "Don't worry that I think badly of you. I think...wonderfully of you. And you're...attracted to me?" He'd been almost certain she was, but the tiny smile she gave him in reply left no doubt at all. He almost exploded again.

"You're *sure* you don't think badly of me?" she whispered.

"Positive," he murmured, capturing her lips once more.

He'd never before kissed a woman who felt or tasted even half as good as Dani did. He began kissing her harder, possessing her mouth with his.

She didn't object. In fact, she kissed him back so deliciously that he could scarcely believe he wasn't dreaming.

With the fraction of his brain that was still functioning, he began to wonder just exactly *how* different things were between men and women in the future. Just *precisely* what Dani had meant by a woman *responding* to a man.

She slid her hands up his back, drawing him so close that he could feel the fullness of her breasts pressing against his chest, could feel the hardness of her nipples. It made him desperately want to possess all of her.

But how could he possibly want her so badly when he knew he couldn't have her? What had happened to his resolve? To his self-control?

Barely able to breathe, he stopped kissing her and made himself draw away a little.

It did no good.

Her arms were circling his waist and she gently rested her cheek against his chest. He still wanted her every bit as much.

"Oh, Dani," he whispered. "Why do you have to be from the wrong time?"

She gazed up at him again, finally whispering, "What if I wasn't?"

He merely shook his head. She *was*, so where was the point in thinking about what might have been?

"What if I wasn't?" she whispered once more.

"I'd want to marry you," he slowly admitted. "I'd want to spend the rest of my life with you. I've fallen in love with you, Dani."

Fresh tears began trickling down her cheeks.

"What?" he murmured, brushing them away. "What's wrong?"

"It's not fair, Karsten. It's just not fair. Because I've fallen in love with you, too."

EXCEPT FOR A LITTLE LIGHT from stray moonbeams, the bedroom was dark. And the cottage was quiet. Not even Czar's breathing was audible.

Dani's mind, though, was spinning far too busily to let her sleep. Enough had happened in one day to fill a book.

First there'd been the arrival of the villagers. Then she'd found herself forced into telling Zanna the truth. Then Karsten had brought Sigismund to the cottage and made her go through the story all over again.

And then, of course, after Sigismund had left . . .

What on earth was she going to do about what had happened with Karsten?

Until today, she'd been convinced that she could handle her feelings for him simply by keeping them to herself. But now that he'd told her he loved her, now that she'd admitted out loud that she loved him . . . it had been like opening Pandora's box.

And the way he'd kissed her good-night would have had her mind spinning even without help from all the other things.

Her brain kept insisting that his being out there in the living room, while she was here in the bedroom, was the only rational arrangement. After all, people from two different centuries weren't supposed to come together at all, let alone *that* way.

But regardless of what her brain was saying, all she could think about was being with him. She wanted just to wrap her arms around him and never let him go.

But she *would* be letting him go. Or, more accurately, she'd be going. Back to where she belonged.

Yet how could she leave him when, with every passing day, he seemed more and more to be her ideal man? On top of being gorgeous, Karsten Nicholae was kind, intelligent, funny and everything else she could ever wish for. Everything, that was, except for the minor detail that he lived in 1850.

She must have unwittingly committed some terrible sin in her brief time on earth. Because if she wasn't being punished for doing something dreadful, why had fate arranged for her to meet Mr. Right in such an impossibly wrong place?

Turning restlessly, she forced her thoughts away from Karsten and began considering the problem of that vampire hunter.

Ion Dobrin was a little ferret of a man. She'd dis-liked him on sight and didn't trust him an inch.

And what if Karsten was right? What if Ion *was* only here on a spy mission—so he could try pinning the vampire label on either Karsten or Sigismund?

Not that she thought he could. That stupid Nicho-lae legend probably didn't have a grain of truth to it. After all, she *knew* Karsten wasn't a vampire. And nobody would ever even wonder about Zanna. And despite her suspicions about Sigismund, she'd never seen a trace of actual evidence.

And now that he'd agreed to let Ion stay here... well, surely no self-respecting vampire would allow a vampire hunter to stay right under his own roof. Es-pecially not one who'd brought along a vampire hunting dog.

At dinner, Ion had told her that Lupus could smell one of the Un-Dead a mile away. And since the dog hadn't shown any interest in either Karsten or Sigis-mund, shouldn't that have been enough to prove to Ion that they weren't vampires?

Of course... Ion might have exaggerated Lupus's talents.

She pounded her pillow a couple of times, pretend-ing it was Ion Dobrin, then closed her eyes and tried her hardest to stop worrying and get to sleep. Gradu-ally, she relaxed and drifted off.

The next thing she knew, a fearsome noise jolted her awake. There were beasts growling... at least two of them.

Instinct had her clutching at the edge of the quilt, pulling it up over her head. But her brain had already switched into adult mode, and trying to make herself invisible was a child's reaction. Hiding under a quilt would be no protection from wild animals.

Heart pounding, she slid her hand beneath the pillow and across the sheet until her fingers found the gun Karsten had given her. Closing her hand around its handle, she eased the quilt down and braved peering through the darkness.

She expected to see black panthers, poised to spring at her. But she saw nothing to account for the vicious noises. All there was at the foot of the bed was a pale, free-floating mist.

Then, before her eyes, it took the form of a man. The corners of his cape were trailing, ghostlike, into the remaining wisps of mist.

"I have come for you," he whispered.

The shiver of terror that seized her would have measured ten on the Richter scale. His voice sounded as if it was echoing hollowly from beyond the grave.

Hands shaking, she raised the revolver and aimed it at the vampire.

Then, suddenly, there was only mist again.

But she'd seen him. And heard him.

After all the time that had passed, she'd started thinking she was safe. But just as he'd promised in the cave, he'd come to her in the darkness. In the middle of the night. When she was alone.

The mist began drifting lazily about the bedroom. She watched it in horrified fascination, resting her hand on her pounding heart and reminding herself she wasn't really alone. Karsten was just in the living room. A scream would bring him running.

She opened her mouth . . . no sound came out. And when she tried to take a deep, calming breath, it caught on the fear in her throat.

But Czar was right in the room with her, she realized, hearing him growl. Turning toward the sound she could see him, his white fur gleaming in the darkness. He was standing beside the bed, hackles raised.

When she looked away from him again the mist had vanished. The vampire was gone . . . for the moment, at least.

Forcing herself out of bed, she hurried over to the window, reaching it just in time to see the shadowy form of a wolf disappearing into the pines.

Trembling, she hugged herself against the cold night breeze that was coming through the open window.

Karsten had told her that vampires could appear as mist or wolves or bats. So far, this one was two for three. Did that mean he'd be back as a bat, to complete the hat trick?

She quickly closed the window.

As it banged shut, she remembered something that sent another shiver through her. The window had been closed and locked when she'd gone to bed. She was certain of it. Which meant that whatever form the vampire chose to take, he could get into her bedroom. So she wasn't any safer in the cottage than in the castle, after all.

Carefully, she latched the window, even though the effort was probably futile.

Czar had trotted across the room to her side and begun to nuzzle her hand, so she nervously stroked his head.

"Good dog," she whispered, glad to discover her voice was back. At least she wouldn't be reduced to using sign language to tell Karsten what had happened.

Karsten. She turned and headed for the living room, desperately needing Karsten to hold her and tell her everything was going to be all right—even if it wasn't true.

From the doorway, she could see his sleeping form in the pale moonlight, his chest slowly rising and falling with each breath.

Crossing quietly to the couch, she knelt down beside him. The sheet was pulled up over his face, hiding it entirely, and she drew it down a few inches.

Then she choked back a startled scream.

It wasn't Karsten on her couch. It was Sigismund.

Chapter Nine

Still clutching the corner of sheet she'd pulled down, Dani stared at Sigismund's face. Then he snorted in his sleep and she dropped the sheet as if it were afire.

What was Sigismund doing on her couch? And where was Karsten?

He'd turned in at the same time she had, just as he did every night. But now he was gone and Sigismund was in his place, fast asleep.

And if Sigismund had slept through that vampire coming into her bedroom and making those horrible, beastly noises, he was an even heavier sleeper than she was. Unless...a nervous little shudder ran through her.

How long had she been standing at the bedroom window after the vampire had vanished? Long enough for it to assume human shape and come into the living room...and get settled on the couch?

But that wouldn't explain why Karsten wasn't here. So, a more logical explanation was that he and Sigismund were up to something together. And whatever it was, they obviously hadn't intended her to know about it.

Of course, the most logical explanations weren't always the right ones.

She eyed Sigismund closely, not able to tell for *sure* whether he was deeply asleep or an excellent actor.

Of course, she *had* finally decided that he was a pretty unlikely vampire suspect. But as long as there was any chance at all, she'd better just leave this hanging for the moment. She'd far rather wait and talk to Karsten about it than wake Sigismund—assuming he wasn't lying there faking.

Czar began to snuffle dangerously near Sigismund's ear, so she wrapped her arms around his furry neck and hugged him to her, then she pushed herself up from the floor and crept back into the bedroom with the dog.

She didn't close the door, though. She didn't *really* think there was much chance that was the vampire lying on her couch. And if the real thing *did* return, and subjected her to more of those terrifying animal noises, she wanted Sigismund to hear them and come running.

On the other hand, if, by some chance, strange vampire things started up in the living room, she'd be able to see what was happening.

The window was still securely locked, and her revolver was lying on the bed where she'd left it. It might not be loaded with silver bullets, the way Karsten's was, but she doubted the vampire could tell that. If he could, he wouldn't have been frightened off when she'd pointed it at him.

She propped the pillows up against the end of the bed so she could see both the window and out into the living room. Then she crawled under the quilt and patted the straw mattress, whispering, "Come on, Czar."

The dog gave a delighted wag of his tail, leapt up and circled until he found a choice spot, then flopped down beside her.

With her gaze fixed on the window, she sat clutching the gun in one hand and absently stroking his fur with the other.

DANI WOKE with such a start she almost screamed.

But there was nothing to scream about. It was morning. Bright daylight was streaming into the bedroom. She'd made it through the night without the vampire returning.

At least, if he *had* made a second visit, she wasn't aware of it.

Anxiously, she ran her fingers down either side of her neck, then felt silly for checking. If she'd been bitten during the night, she'd probably be dead.

Czar was still on the bed and he stretched lazily, then jumped down, almost knocking the gun onto the floor in the process. Dani moved it to the safety of the bedside table, then pulled on her robe and headed through the open doorway into the living room.

There, asleep on the couch, lay Karsten.

Glancing at him, she wondered for a moment if last night could possibly be explained away as a nightmare. Maybe the vampire hadn't really appeared. Maybe she'd only dreamed that she'd come out to the living room and found Sigismund in Karsten's place.

But no. If she hadn't actually gotten up during the night, how could she account for having fallen back to sleep with her gun at the ready? Or for the bedroom door being open this morning? Or for why Czar had slept on the bed? She'd never invited him before.

She continued over to the front door and let the dog out, then quietly started back to the bedroom, wanting a little time to herself before Karsten woke.

If she hoped to get a completely honest explanation from him, she needed to give her questions some thought, rather than just blurting them out any old way.

She closed the bedroom door, chose a dress from the wardrobe, then tossed her robe onto the bed and tugged her nightgown off over her head, thinking all the while.

But by the time she was fully dressed, she'd decided there was no magic way to broach the subject. She'd just have to play things by ear.

She dug her waist pack out from the back of the wardrobe, spritzed a little perfume behind her ears, returned the pack to its hiding place and closed the wardrobe door.

Then she turned away from it and almost went into cardiac arrest.

A man was staring boldly through the bedroom window at her.

Ion Dobrin.

His ferrety face lit up with a smile when he realized that she'd seen him. She didn't smile back. She simply stood glaring daggers at him.

How long had that sneaky little voyeur been standing out there watching her? The entire time she'd been getting dressed?

If he'd seen her naked . . . oh, heavens, even worse than naked was if he'd seen her in her twentieth-century underwear. She should have gone with Danica Radulesco's corsets and cotton bloomers, after all. Because if Ion had seen her silk panties and sports bra, what would he think? That wasn't hard to imagine, and the last person she wanted wondering if she had any secrets was a professional spy.

He tapped quietly on the glass, beckoning to her.

"I have to talk to you," he whispered when she opened the window. "It's most important. May I come in?"

Reluctantly, she nodded, managing not to snarl at him. Telling him what she thought of his playing Peeping Tom wouldn't get her anywhere. But maybe, by talking to him, she'd be able to tell whether he'd realized there was something strange about her or not. "Go around to the front door and—"

"No, no, my dear lady. I don't want to wake Master Nicholae. We must speak in private. So I'll just climb in through your window, if I may."

Uncertainly, she backed away from it.

The man knew Karsten was asleep in the living room. No, he'd said *Master* Nicholae, so maybe he thought it was Sigismund in there. Whichever, though, it made her suspect that he'd already learned a lot about what went on at Castle Ceistra.

He wriggled in through the open window, then smoothed his gray hair and smiled at her again. That made his eyes narrower, which made him look even more ferretlike.

At dinner last night, she'd noticed how badly he smelled. And that his breath would likely knock a vampire off a fresh kill. But in the dim light of the castle, she hadn't noticed the red carbuncle on the side of his nose. It had a single black hair growing from its center.

All in all, Ion Dobrin was one of the last men in the world she'd normally allow in her bedroom.

"What do you want?" she asked him.

"Perhaps we could sit?" he suggested, already heading for the bed.

"I prefer to stand." She leaned against the wall, crossing her arms over her chest.

"As you wish." Ion perched on the edge of the bed, and looked over at her with a worried expression. "Has anything unusual happened since you've been staying at Castle Ceistra?"

"Unusual?" she repeated, buying time. She had to decide whether or not to tell him about the vampire appearing last night. After all, he *was* a vampire hunter, so she probably should. But she hadn't trusted him *before* his Peeping Tom routine, and she trusted him even less now. So maybe she shouldn't say a word until she'd talked to Karsten.

"Unusual? Out of the ordinary? Frightening?" Ion was saying.

"Well, I did see the vampire," she admitted. "But that was a long time ago. Just after I got here, he came into a cave I was in and—"

"Yes, yes, Mistress Zanna told me about that. But more recently?"

"Zanna told you about that?" Dani could feel an army of butterflies invading her stomach.

"Yes. I had a long, long talk with her this morning. We're both early risers."

"Oh." That certainly explained how Ion had learned things so fast. But how *much* had Zanna told him?

"And what all did Zanna have to say?" she tried.

"Oh, many things. Many things. She does like to talk. But... my dear lady, I haven't come to discuss Mistress Zanna. I've come to warn you. You seem oblivious to the perilous situation you're in. Do you not realize that one of the Nicholaes is likely a vampire?"

"That's not true. It's just a ridiculous legend."

"No, I'm afraid it may be much more than that. So it worries me that you allow one of them to stay with you in the night."

"I don't think that's any of your concern."

Ion gave her a long, slow shrug. "Romulus Teodescu has hired me to determine who the vampire is. But if I can prevent it from killing again, before I am absolutely certain of its identity, I would prefer to. Especially when its next victim could be a beautiful woman."

The butterflies in Dani's stomach began to multiply at an alarming rate.

"Your dog," she said, trying to retain her grip on logical reason. "You told me your dog could smell a vampire a mile away. And I didn't see him paying particular attention to anyone in the castle last night."

"No, *you* wouldn't see it. Lupus is well trained. He seldom reacts enough for most people to notice. And sometimes his reactions are not what most people would take them to be. When he growled at that servant, for example."

"What servant?"

"Oh, I guess you weren't there. Yesterday, when I first arrived. The stable master it was."

"Letcha?"

"Yes, that's the name. Lupus only growled at him because he knew Letcha wanted to take him away from me—take him off to the stable."

"You're sure that's all it was?" Dani held her breath, waiting for Ion's reply. Letcha had been giving her the creeps since the first moment she'd seen him. She'd never thought about *him* possibly being the vampire, but now that she was—

"Yes, I always know what Lupus is saying."

"But . . . this thing with the vampire, Mr. Dobrin. I mean, people thinking it's one of the Nicholaes because Ernos was attacked in the castle. Couldn't the vampire be someone in the castle who isn't a Nicholae?"

"That's an interesting thought," Ion said slowly.

Dani was just about to press him on *how* interesting when he beat her with a question of his own.

"But let me ask you this," he said. "Do you have any idea where Karsten Nicholae goes in the middle of the night?"

"Goes?" she said, the word coming out a little squeaky. "What do you mean, where he goes?"

"Ahh . . . you aren't even aware of his nocturnal activities. You must sleep soundly."

Dani resisted the impulse to nod, but, of course, Ion was right. Last night was the first time since she'd been here that she hadn't slept straight through. Which meant . . . oh, Lord, that meant last night might not have been a unique occurrence.

In fact, now that she thought about it, she'd frequently seen Karsten checking that old-fashioned pocket watch of his if they talked very late into the night. Was that because he'd had somewhere to go? An appointment to keep?

For all she knew, Sigismund had been taking Karsten's place regularly. But, then, what had Karsten been doing?

"There's no doubt Master Nicholae is active after darkness falls," Ion went on. "Romulus Teodescu has had a man watching Castle Ceistra's gate each night. And Master Karsten frequently leaves the grounds at two o'clock in the morning. The time is apparently quite consistent.

"He rides off on his big black horse. Black. The devil's color. Does that not strike you as interesting?"

"Karsten leaves and goes where?" Dani demanded, ignoring Ion's question. She didn't give a damn about the color of Karsten's horse, but she definitely wanted to know what he did at night.

Ion shrugged again. "No one has followed him. That would be too dangerous if he actually *is* ... well, why would any mortal man go riding in the night? One seldom hunts for *animals* in the darkness."

Dani's adrenaline had begun pumping so hard she could feel it racing through her body. After finding Karsten gone last night, she could hardly doubt that Ion was right about his going out some place. But where? And why?

Whatever he was up to, though, it certainly wasn't hunting for human victims. "Mr. Dobrin, I don't know what Karsten does when he goes out, but I can assure you he isn't the vampire."

"Oh?"

"Yes. When Zanna told you about my seeing the vampire, didn't she tell you that Karsten was with me? That we saw it together?"

"Yes. Yes, she did."

"Well, then?"

Ion gave her a skeptical look.

"Mr. Dobrin, I'm aware a vampire can appear in various forms, but surely you aren't trying to imply that it can appear as two individuals at the same time."

"No, naturally not. But..." Ion slowly shook his head. "Oh, my dear, dear lady. I do believe it hasn't even occurred to you. But who is to say there's not more than one of the Un-Dead in the area? Or that Master Karsten didn't have someone follow the two of you that day? Someone who came into the cave and *impersonated* a vampire, in order to convince you it couldn't be he, himself?"

Dani simply stared at the vampire hunter. He was right. Neither of those possibilities had even crossed her mind.

"OF COURSE," Ion Dobrin continued, "mine is a most deliberate process. I take my time."

Dani nodded, thinking that he certainly did. It seemed like an hour since he'd climbed in through her window and he was still talking.

"I have to determine guilt beyond any shadow of doubt. And I haven't entirely ruled out Master Sigismund or Mistress Zanna."

"Zanna?" Dani would have laughed if she weren't so upset.

"Oh, one cannot be too quick to dismiss a woman. They are the most cunning of the Un-Dead. And she could just as easily have hired someone to impersonate a vampire as Master Karsten. But there *is* a chance you're right about the Nicholae legend being ridiculous. A chance that our vampire is not a Nicholae at all. It seems a faint chance, though."

Dani simply nodded again. The longer Ion talked, the more worried she'd become. Clearly, he was almost positive that *Karsten* was the vampire.

But Ion was wrong.

Oh, he'd definitely thrown her for a minute, when he'd mentioned those possibilities of his. But the idea of Karsten hiring someone to impersonate a vampire was ludicrous. And, even if there were a hundred Un-Dead in the area, Karsten wasn't one of them.

In the short time she'd been here, she'd come to know Karsten so well that she'd fallen desperately in love with him. And she certainly couldn't have fallen in love with a vampire.

"So..." she said at last, "this *deliberate* process. How long do you think it will take you to establish for sure who the vampire is?"

"Oh, it will take some time. Probably, until after the hunter's moon, at least. I told my wife not to expect me back in Timisoara until well after that."

After the hunter's moon, Dani silently repeated. That meant she'd be gone before Ion came to his conclusion. But she couldn't go without knowing that Karsten would be all right. She had to make sure this was straightened out before she left.

A sudden knocking on the bedroom door made her jump.

"Dani?" Karsten called. "Dani, aren't you awake yet?"

"It would be best if he didn't know I was here," Ion whispered quickly. "If you get him away from the door, I'll leave immediately."

Without waiting for her to reply, he crouched down beside the bed, where he'd be out of sight from the doorway.

"Dani?" Karsten called again.

"Coming," she called back. "Just a second."

She started across the room, her mind racing full tilt. Karsten was going to have to explain to Ion Dobrin what he did when he went out at night. Because, if he didn't . . .

When she opened the door, Karsten smiled one of his sexiest smiles. Usually, they made her feel weak-kneed, but at the moment she was too upset to feel anything else.

Then she caught her gaze pausing on Karsten's canines. Her subconscious must have wanted her to check them, and that realization produced a rush of guilt.

What Ion had been trying to convince her of simply couldn't be true. She was certain of that. So why did she have to reassure herself that Karsten's teeth were all normal-size? And why did seeing that they were make her feel better?

She had to get a grip on her imagination or she'd be thinking all kinds of crazy things.

Stepping out of the bedroom and reclosing the door, she put her finger to her lips, grabbed Karsten's hand, and dragged him to the couch.

"Don't I get a good-morning kiss?" he said, sinking down beside her.

"Shh," she whispered. "Ion Dobrin is in the bedroom."

"What?" Karsten demanded angrily. "Why that little . . . I'll go and—"

"Shh," she cautioned him again, grabbing his other hand to keep him sitting. "Just stay here and listen."

"What's he doing in there?"

"He's been telling me . . . Karsten, where did you go last night?"

His face became a mask. He took his hands from hers and rubbed his jaw, as if that would produce an answer.

"What are you talking about?" he finally said.

"I am talking," she told him, enunciating precisely and glaring at the same time, "about waking up and finding Sigismund asleep on this couch instead of you. What was he doing here?"

"Making sure you were safe. Making sure the vampire didn't come. What the hell did you think he was doing here?"

Dani hesitated, realizing she should tell Karsten the vampire *had* come. But that could wait. The problem with Ion Dobrin couldn't.

"Karsten, my question wasn't really about why Sigismund was here. It was about why you *weren't* here. Where *were* you? Ion Dobrin knows that you ride out on Ebony in the middle of the night."

Karsten swore, then said, "How does he know that?"

"Because the mayor has had the castle under surveillance."

"The *mayor!* That slimy toad shouldn't be the mayor of a herd of goats. But nobody knows where I go."

Dani wasn't sure whether that was a statement or a question, but she shook her head. "No, nobody's ever followed you. But the point is that Ion thinks you're the vampire. So you have to explain to him where you *do* go. What you're doing out there in the dark."

"I can't tell him."

"What?"

"I said, I can't tell him."

"I *heard* what you said. But you *have* to tell him."

"I certainly don't. It's none of his business, and I have no intention of telling him. Or anyone else, for that matter."

Dani took a deep breath. This was a side of Karsten she hadn't seen before. Irrational and pigheaded.

"Karsten," she said, trying to sound perfectly calm and reasonable. "What if Ion makes up his mind that you're *definitely* the vampire? What if he tells the villagers that?"

Karsten shrugged, trying to look unconcerned. She knew better, though.

"What would happen?" she prodded.

"Well...I guess they'd decide whether they thought he was right or not."

She bit back an extremely sarcastic remark. They were talking about a vampire hunter whom the villagers themselves had hired. Romulus Teodescu had arranged for Ion to come all the way from Timbuktu or whatever darn town he was from. And if he told them that Karsten was their man—or their vampire, as the case would be—the odds that they'd believe him were probably one-hundred percent.

"And if they *did* think Ion was right?" she pressed.

"I guess they'd want to deal with the matter."

"You mean they'd try to kill you."

"Well . . . yes, but that isn't going to happen. Everything will turn out just fine."

"You don't *know* that."

"No? Dani, if the villagers ever became *really* convinced there was a vampire living in the castle, they'd storm it. Burn it down. And you told me yourself that, years from now, Sigismund will be living in Castle Ceistra as Count Nicholae. You said you knew his name from your family's history."

"So?" she asked, not getting the point.

"So we know the castle doesn't get stormed. Doesn't get burned. So everything will be fine."

Dani stared at Karsten in disbelief. "Do you think I'm an idiot? You aren't *actually* trying to pass that off as logical, are you? Who says they'd have to storm the castle to kill you? Maybe they'd catch you out riding in the middle of the night. What I know from my family history only takes care of your brother's future, not yours."

"I can take care of my own future, Dani. Nobody's going to kill me."

"No?" she snapped. He was being so infuriating she wanted to smack him. "Well, I got an awfully different impression, listening to that little ferret in the bedroom. Karsten, either you tell Ion Dobrin what you're up to at night or you're going to be in big, big trouble.''

"You're overreacting, Dani.''

She clenched her fists in anger. That wasn't an 1850 word. That was a word from the future. One *she'd* used and then had to explain to him.

And she *wasn't* overreacting. If she couldn't make Karsten see reason, Ion Dobrin was going to finger him as the vampire. Then the villagers would kill him.

The mere thought of Karsten being killed made her throat tighten. She might be mad at him, but she still loved him.

She'd finally found the one man in the world for her. And even though she'd found him in the wrong century, she didn't want him to die. What she wanted was...

Well, what she *really* wanted was probably as ridiculous as it was unlikely to happen. And she hadn't had enough time to think it through thoroughly, hadn't come anywhere near to deciding if she should even say a word.

Besides, if she was being deep-down honest, she had to admit that a tiny speck of doubt about Karsten had resurfaced in her mind—thanks to Ion Dobrin.

She truly despised that little man.

She despised him, but she loved Karsten. So letting her imagination try to make her wonder about Karsten again was absolutely ridiculous. She simply wasn't going to wonder for a second.

Karsten was the man she loved and he wasn't a vampire. Period.

And if Ion didn't think he'd be completing his vampire report until after the hunter's moon . . .

She took a long, deep breath and made a split second decision that could change her entire life.

"Karsten, everything I've told you about the future . . . you seem so fascinated by it all."

"I am. Who wouldn't be?"

"Well, it's occurred to me that . . . you and I . . . what we were kind of talking about yesterday . . ."

"What?"

She screwed up her courage and let the words rush out before she lost her nerve. "About spending the rest of our lives together. Maybe it *could* be possible. Karsten, what if you came with me when I leave?"

He looked at her for a long, long, minute, then said, "No. There's no way I could go with you. But you could stay here with me, Dani. You could stay here and marry me."

Chapter Ten

Dani simply stared at Karsten, not knowing what to say.

"Dani?" he murmured, taking her hands in his. "Dani, I asked you to marry me. I love you."

"Yes . . . yes, I heard. And I love you, too," she whispered, her head spinning.

"God, you don't know how fantastic that makes me feel. We can announce the betrothal right away. Just as soon as my parents return from Bucharest."

He moved to kiss her, but she pressed her fingers against his lips. "Karsten, wait. I need a minute to think."

Actually, she needed at least an entire week to think.

Making a conscious effort not to let her mind go off in twenty different directions, she focused on Karsten's proposal. The idea of living the rest of her life in 1850 was mind-boggling on its own, without the added complication of vampires and that vampire hunter. But there *were* those added complications.

Unless Karsten straightened things out with Ion Dobrin, he'd end up telling the Biertan villagers that the man she loved was the vampire. Then Karsten would be as good as dead.

Of course, to prevent that part from happening, all she had to do was convince Karsten to tell Ion what he was up to in the middle of the night. Then Ion would concentrate on looking for the *real* vampire.

But *all she had to do* was easier said than done— now that she'd discovered how pigheaded Karsten could be.

And not all the obstacles lay in this century, either. There was one back where she belonged that she couldn't possibly forget.

"Dani?" Karsten said quietly.

She gazed into the blue depth of his eyes, trying not to think that losing him would be the worst torture imaginable. "Karsten, I do love you. So very, very much. But I can't stay in 1850."

"Dani, you can. It—"

"No, let me explain. I *have* to go back. Because, by now, my parents will be certain I'm dead. When a woman simply vanishes... well, they'll have concluded the worst. That I was abducted. Raped. Murdered. I just couldn't stay here, knowing they'd be believing that for the rest of their lives."

"Yes," he said slowly. "Yes, I can understand that you'll have to see them again. But you could come back to me after you've explained things to them."

"I... but it would be almost a year before I could come back. The spell to get me here again wouldn't work until the next harvest moon."

"I can wait a year, Dani. I'd wait forever for you."

"But..." Oh, Lord, so much could happen in an entire year—especially given the fix Karsten was in.

Unless he convinced Ion Dobrin he wasn't the vampire, she'd come back in a year to find he'd been killed.

Her suggestion had made far more sense. If Karsten went to her time, it wouldn't matter whether anyone here thought he was the vampire or not.

But he'd said there was no way he'd go.

Mentally, she raced through all the objections he could possibly have to living in her world, and tried to come up with counter-arguments.

"You know, Karsten," she said at last, "you didn't really take time to consider coming with me when I leave. But we shouldn't just rule it out. I'm sure you'd make out fine. You're a natural linguist. Every time I use a word in English, you pick it up right away. So you'd be speaking perfect English in no time. And—"

"Dani, it isn't that I don't think I'd make out all right. At least, that isn't the main problem. It's that I *can't* leave. I've got an extremely important reason for having to stay here."

"What?" she demanded. What reason could possibly be more important than their future together?

Karsten slowly shook his head. "I'm sorry, but I can't tell you."

With only a slightly exaggerated motion, she removed her hands from his. Then she waited, giving him a chance to realize how ridiculous his statement had been.

He simply sat looking at her.

"Karsten," she said at last, "you can't *not* tell me. I need to know your reason. I need to know all the facts."

"Not this one. It's something I can't tell anyone."

"I'm not *anyone*. I'm the woman you *claim* you love."

"I *do* love you. But there's no need for you to know the reason. It doesn't involve you."

"Doesn't *involve* me?" she snapped, aware of how angry she sounded but not caring. "How can it not involve me when you're asking me to give up my entire life? When you're asking me to live way back in the past, because you *say* there's some reason you can't go to the future with me? How can you possibly figure it doesn't involve me? Karsten, get real!"

Karsten rubbed his jaw uneasily. He'd never had a woman lash out at him before. Of course, he knew women in her world were more aggressive. Dani had told him an awful lot about how things had changed between men and women over the years. And she'd explained all about how couples interacted in the future, about their *relationships,* as she called them.

But he hadn't quite realized...hell, she looked as if she'd like to rip his heart out.

Even though he damned well wasn't going to tell her what she wanted to know, she seemed so angry that he'd better try to...*communicate,* that was her word. Yes, he'd better try to communicate a little, because he distinctly remembered her saying that to make those relationships work properly, people sometimes had to compromise and give more than they wanted to.

"Dani, look, I'll tell you this much. My having to stay here has to do with my going out at night. So...well, there, now I've kind of explained both things to you. But that's all I can say, okay?"

"No, it's not okay! And you haven't explained a single thing. Why not? Don't you trust me with a secret?"

"Ahh..."

"You don't? No, I can see it in your eyes, you don't! How can you say you love me when you don't trust me?"

"I *do* trust you, but..."

"But what?"

He cleared his throat. He didn't seem to be doing too well, here, but he also remembered her saying that honesty was essential in relationships.

"But what?" she snapped again.

"Well...all right, to be honest with you, I guess the problem is that I keep remembering you told Zanna you were from the future. After I'd warned you and warned you not to."

"She was pointing a damned rifle at me!"

Karsten shrugged unhappily. He *definitely* wasn't doing too well, here. He might have grasped some of the theory about this relationship thing, but he was obviously in need of a whole lot more practice.

He was almost afraid to open his mouth again, but then he had a thought. Dani prided herself on being a logical thinker, so didn't a little logic have to be worth a shot?

"What if somebody pointed a loaded rifle at you again?" he tried.

It had seemed like a perfectly reasonable question to him, but she apparently didn't think so. Without another word, she stood up and stomped off to the bedroom, slamming the door behind her.

Karsten was still trying to decide if he'd only make things worse by going after her when the bedroom door flew open again.

One look at Dani's face told him she'd gone from angry to frightened.

"What?" he asked.

She made a helpless little motion with her hands, gesturing him to follow her back into the bedroom. He shoved himself off the couch and raced over.

When he barreled through the bedroom doorway, Dani was standing in front of the open wardrobe.

She looked over at him with fear in her eyes. "Karsten, I'm almost positive I closed the wardrobe door when I finished dressing. And when I came in here it was open. And...I'm not entirely certain, but I think that Ion looked through my things. My things from the future, I mean. I think I put my waist pack down on top of my sneakers, earlier. But when I just looked, it was to the side."

"That damned little snake," Karsten muttered. He'd gotten so involved in arguing with Dani that he'd forgotten all about Ion being in here. "Where is he?" he asked, glancing at her again.

"He's gone," she said, not looking over. She was busy digging something out of the back of the wardrobe.

"They're still here," she murmured, turning and holding Danica Radulesco's open jewel case out to show him that the jewelry was safe.

"I thought he might have taken something, but these are the only valuable things in here. At least he's not a thief. But, oh, Karsten, we got awfully loud, didn't we. Maybe he heard us talking about the future . . . or maybe he saw me with my pack earlier, before I put it away."

"You had it out when he was in here with you?"

"No. He was looking in through the window. But I didn't even think about his maybe having seen it at the time. I was too worried about his having seen my underwear."

"*What?*"

"Karsten, don't yell. But I've been wearing my own underwear. And it isn't like anything people in 1850 have ever seen. It . . . doesn't cover much. If Ion saw it, he'd really wonder about me."

For half a second, Karsten was overwhelmed with curiosity. He'd give all the flagons of wine in the castle cellar to see Dani in underwear that didn't cover much.

Then his anger returned and washed the curiosity from his mind. If *he* couldn't see her in her underwear and that scrawny vampire hunter had . . .

"Dani, let me get this straight. Was Ion standing outside the window while you were getting dressed? He saw you half-naked?"

"*Half* . . . well, I don't know how long he'd been standing there . . . how much he saw."

"What? You mean he could have seen more? He could have seen you *completely* naked?"

"I don't know."

Karsten could feel his blood heating from simmer to boil. "Well, let's just go and ask that little worm what he saw! And then I think I'll kill him."

DANI EYED KARSTEN uneasily as she spoke. She might have kept him from racing off to kill Ion Dobrin by filling him in about the vampire's visit, but he didn't look any less angry.

"Then, once it was gone," she concluded, "I ran into the living room to tell you. And that's when I found Sigismund sleeping here on the couch, instead of you."

Karsten shook his head. "Right in the cottage. The vampire, right in the cottage. God, Dani, it could have gotten you."

"It didn't, though. But when Ion showed up this morning...I didn't say anything to him about its having come, Karsten. I wasn't sure if I should or not. What do you think?"

"I think I'm going to order him the hell out of Castle Ceistra. So there's no point in telling him anything."

Dani watched Karsten pace across the living room once more. He definitely wasn't any less angry at Ion, but now he was worried about her safety again, to boot.

Not that she didn't think there was every reason to worry. But maybe if he'd *been* here last night when the vampire had showed up, if he'd been here, where he was supposed to be, instead of off wherever...

"Karsten?" she finally said, unable to stop herself. "Karsten, we didn't finish talking about last night. You never did tell me where you go on Ebony."

He ran his fingers through his hair, saying, "Dani, let's not get into that again, okay? It wouldn't be safe for you to know, so I just can't tell you."

"You mean you just *won't* tell me," she snapped. "You won't tell me and you won't tell Ion, either. And if you stick to that plan you're going to end up dead—

with your head cut off and a stake through your heart."

"Don't forget the part where my mouth gets stuffed with garlic," he muttered sarcastically.

"Karsten, that is *not* funny! Don't you see that it's only logical for Ion to think you're the vampire? He knows you go off in the middle of the night, exactly the time the vampire's out killing people. So what's the obvious conclusion? Dammit, if you keep on being so pigheaded about not telling people the truth...how do even *I* know for sure that you aren't the vampire?"

Karsten stopped pacing long enough to glare at her. She glared right back.

"You actually believe that?" he demanded.

"I didn't say I believed it. I said, how could I be *sure* you aren't."

"Well, if you're not sure, I don't know why in the world we were talking about getting married. In fact, I don't know why we should bother talking at all." Karsten turned on his heel and stormed toward the door.

"Where are you going?"

"To find Ion Dobrin and kick him out of the castle. In fact, I might kick him halfway to Biertan Village."

"Karsten, wait, I—"

"And I don't need your help to do it."

Ignoring that remark, Dani pushed herself up off the couch and hurried out after him. She wished she'd never opened her mouth about Ion watching her through the window. Or about suspecting he'd looked through her things.

If she'd thought about it for half a minute she wouldn't have. Because she'd have realized Karsten would react this way, and angering Ion would be the worst thing he could do.

"Karsten, listen to me," she said as they started through the pines. "If you kick Ion halfway to Biertan Village, you know what he'll do, don't you? He'll run the rest of the way there and tell everyone you *are* the vampire."

"Then maybe I should go back to my original plan and kill the little bastard."

"Oh, wouldn't that be clever? Really, really clever. Karsten, get ahold of yourself and think. Where would a major confrontation with Ion get us? Nowhere. Whatever you accused him of he'd simply deny. And I'm not *certain* he went through my things. And I don't know *for sure* that he was watching me when I was..."

"When you weren't wearing any clothes."

"I'm not *at all* sure how long he was standing outside that window. Maybe it was only two seconds."

"Or maybe it was ten minutes."

"Karsten, *please?* Let's just have a reasonable conversation with him. Maybe we can find out if he saw anything. Or if Zanna told him anything she shouldn't have."

"Zanna?" Karsten stopped in his tracks. "Zanna's been telling him things?"

"Oh. I guess I forgot to mention that, but yes. He said they had a long talk this morning."

"Terrific," Karsten muttered. "Just what we need. You'd better check with her and find out what she said."

"The first chance I get. But I still think we should go slow and easy with Ion. Simply try to sound him out and see if he suspects there's anything strange about me."

"And if he does?"

"Let's just start with *reasonable* and take it from there. Please?"

Karsten's shrug told her he'd at least give some thought to that approach, then he started walking again.

"Okay," he said eventually. "I'm not sure I can hold my temper around him, but I'll try. You get the conversation going, and maybe we *can* have a nice, quiet, reasonable talk. *Then* I'll decide whether to kill him or not."

"All right." Dani began breathing a little easier. "And Karsten?" She reached for his hand as they neared the edge of the pines.

He stopped walking and turned to her, gazing deep into her eyes. "What?"

"The good-morning kiss you mentioned earlier? We never did get to it."

That made him smile... one of his sexiest smiles. Then he wrapped his arms around her waist and drew her close. "How could we ever have forgotten about something like this," he whispered, bending to kiss her.

It was a long, hot, bone-melting kiss that made her want to turn around and drag him straight back to the cottage. But hadn't she told herself a million times, that the way things were, getting *totally* involved with Karsten would be a serious mistake?

"Dani?" he murmured, his breath warm against her lips.

"Mmm?"

"Dani, you *will* come back to me, won't you? You *will* come back to marry me? I couldn't live without you."

"Oh, Karsten." She rested her cheek against his chest, listening to the solid beating of his heart, not sure she could live without him, either.

"Dani?"

"We've still got over a week until the hunter's moon," she whispered. "We'll work things out."

He looked down at her and nodded slowly, but she couldn't tell whether he believed her or not. Small wonder, when she didn't even know whether she believed herself.

"What about the vampire last night?" she asked as they started toward the castle again. "Should I tell Ion it was here?"

Karsten walked a few yards in silence, then said, "Yeah, I guess maybe you'd better. It might be smart to make him figure that we really are cooperating with him because...dammit, Dani, you might be at as much risk from that character now as I am. I mean, what if he did see you in your strange underwear? What if he actually did look at all those unbelievable things of yours? Or what if Zanna said something stupid about your being from the future? What do you think he'd conclude?"

She didn't hazard a guess, because she suspected the answer was that Ion would conclude she was a witch. And if she was right, she didn't want to hear Karsten confirm her suspicion.

WHEN THEY REACHED the castle they found that Ion was in the library—with Sigismund and a man Dani hadn't seen before.

"Come in," Sigismund said. His welcoming gesture was obviously meant for Karsten alone.

Dani pretended she didn't realize that and followed along into the room.

"We're just planning our strategy for finding the vampire," Sigismund went on. "Romulus was kind enough to come up from the village to help us."

Sigismund managed to keep the sarcasm out of his voice, but not off his face. Only Dani and Karsten, though, were in a position to see his expression.

Dani glanced from Sigismund to the stranger he'd referred to as Romulus. Apparently, this was the illustrious mayor of Biertan Village.

She waited, expecting to be introduced, then remembered she was supposed to be Danica Radulesco, who had known Romulus Teodescu only too well.

He was staring straight at her, so she gave him a small smile, not at all certain how the real Danica would have greeted him.

He was about Sigismund's age and build, but those were the only points of resemblance. Unlike the blond-haired, blue-eyed Nicholaes, Romulus had long dark hair and brown eyes.

If his hair were clean, instead of hanging in greasy strands, and if he had shaved, he might not have been bad-looking. But he was sporting a full beard that contained obvious remnants of his breakfast—and, quite possibly, she decided, last night's dinner.

It wasn't hard to see why Danica Radulesco had written in her diary that she'd rather marry a baboon.

"I'd heard you were back, of course, Danica," he finally said. "But it's been a long time since I've seen you."

"Yes . . . a long time." Fleetingly, she recalled that in addition to being mayor, Romulus also owned the Boar's Head Tavern. So she doubted the *long time* was actually the entire year since Danica Radulesco had fled to Walachia.

Romulus had probably seen her the night she'd arrived—when she'd been drugged and lying on a table in his very own establishment. As owner of the place, she doubted he'd have missed the stake-through-the-heart party the villagers had thrown there in her honor.

"I'd like to speak to you for a minute, Danica," Romulus said. "I happened across some very interesting things, and I'd like to talk to you about them."

Her heart nervously skipped a beat as he started across the library. There was something in the way he was eyeing her that made her very uncomfortable. She really didn't want to talk to him. Danica Radulesco might have been able to discuss whatever interesting things he'd come across, but *she* wouldn't have a clue.

Before Romulus reached her, though, Karsten said, "Actually, if you wouldn't mind, Romulus, Dani and I are anxious to talk to Ion."

Romulus stopped midstride and glanced back at the vampire hunter.

Ion smiled, obviously pleased to be sought out.

"Perhaps we could step outside?" Karsten added, motioning him toward the door.

Ignoring Sigismund's annoyed glare, Dani followed Karsten and Ion out of the library and along the hallway to the spacious entrance foyer.

"Well?" Ion said expectantly when they stopped.

Dani cleared her throat. Karsten had said *she* should get things started, but she wished they'd worked out their plan in a little more detail. Maybe, though, if she was ambiguous enough, she'd get Ion to volunteer something useful.

"I mentioned to Karsten that you'd come by the cottage to talk this morning," she began. "And we just wondered if by any chance you saw anything...strange after I left you in the bedroom."

"Strange?"

She waited, hoping the silence would work for her. It did.

"I saw nothing at all," Ion finally offered. "As soon as you went out to the other room, I left. Immediately. As I told you I would.

"I hope," he added, turning to Karsten, "you didn't think it unseemly of me to go in through the bedroom window. But Mistress Zanna had told me you'd be asleep in the living room and I didn't want to disturb you."

"That was very thoughtful of you," Karsten said.

Dani shot him a quick smile for sounding so polite, then looked back at Ion.

"But strange?" he was saying. "Exactly what did you mean by strange?"

"Well...ahh..." Now where did she go? She certainly couldn't ask him if he'd seen her underwear. Or her credit cards or modern watch.

"Well," she tried, "I thought it was possible you'd seen an apparition...because I saw one last night. Right in that bedroom. I was just going to tell you about it this morning when Karsten interrupted us."

"An apparition?" Ion said, leaning forward. His breath would have driven a vampire back to its lair.

She took a step back, trying not to breathe. "Well, actually, I think it was the vampire."

Ion's face lit up with a delighted smile. "Really?"

"Yes . . . I definitely think so."

Ion hung on every word as she recounted the entire story.

"Oh, my," he murmured when she'd finished. "Oh, my, oh, my. This is very good news. Now that he's come to you once, I'm sure we can expect him back."

"That's *good* news?" Dani said. It certainly wasn't how she'd classify the prospect of a return visit from a vampire.

"Oh, yes, good news indeed," Ion assured her. "And I think this means a change in our plans," he added, turning to Karsten once more. "Rather than going out to hunt the vampire, I think we'd be wiser to lay a trap right here in the castle grounds."

"Using Dani as bait? I don't like that idea at all. I think—"

"Don't be silly," Ion interrupted, waving his hand airily. "I can't tell you the details of what I'll do, because vampire hunters are sworn to secrecy about their methods. But Dani will be perfectly safe. After all, I *am* Transylvania's foremost vampire hunter."

The way he drew himself up to his full height of five foot three, she half expected trumpets to sound.

"Now, come along back to the library," he told Karsten. "We must tell your brother and Romulus about this."

Dani glanced uncertainly at Karsten. They hadn't found out a darned thing from Ion. Maybe he'd gone out the bedroom window immediately, as he'd claimed. Or maybe he'd taken time to check out every single item in the wardrobe. And obviously, if he *had* been playing Peeping Tom while she'd gotten dressed, it was the last thing he'd admit to.

But at least he thought Karsten was being cooperative. And if the *real* vampire did show up again . . .

Just the thought of that made her shiver. But, by laying a trap, Ion might establish that it was neither Karsten nor Sigismund . . . neither Karsten nor Sigismund *nor Zanna*, she corrected herself.

"One cannot be too quick to dismiss a woman," Ion had said earlier.

The remark had seemed absurd, though, especially in reference to someone like Zanna.

But regardless of that, if Ion could prove the vampire definitely wasn't a Nicholae, it would be worth having to face the creature one more time.

"Dani?" Karsten said. "Why don't you try to find Zanna? Ask her about that *thing*."

She nodded. That *thing*, of course, being Zanna's long conversation with Ion this morning.

It was past the normal breakfast time, but Zanna sometimes lingered over her tea, so Dani headed across the foyer and into the dining room.

The silver tea service and two clean cups and saucers were sitting at one end of the enormous table, along with a cloth-covered basket. The aroma told her it contained some of the delicious biscuits the new cook had been making each morning.

There was no sign of anyone, though, so Dani wandered toward the kitchen.

Tesia, the woman who'd taken over cooking duties from Ernos's wife, loved to bake. And Zanna had such a sweet tooth that she'd been checking out the kitchen regularly, so she wouldn't miss first crack at something good.

And sure enough, she was there—all alone, standing by the stove with her back to the door.

"Zanna?" Dani said.

Zanna made a startled little noise and whirled around, dropping the cup she'd been holding. The china smashed into smithereens when it hit the stone floor.

Dani stared at the floor, mesmerized by the dark red liquid oozing into a puddle among the broken shards. Then she realized what it was and her eyes flashed to Zanna's mouth.

Her lips were blood red.

Chapter Eleven

Dani stood rooted to the floor, unable to believe her eyes, while Zanna leapt into action.

"My, but you frightened me," she murmured, grabbing a cloth and kneeling to wipe up the mess. "And I'm so clumsy sometimes."

The cloth began turning from white to red as she sopped up the blood.

"Tesia?" she called. "Tesia?"

The new cook came hurrying in from the pantry.

"Tesia, I'm sorry. I've made a mess here."

"I'll take care of it, ma'am. No need for you to do that."

"Well, there's broken china, so do be careful. I waited tea for you," she added, smiling at Dani as she stood up.

Dani glanced at the discolored cloth once more, then back at Zanna. She was still smiling brightly.

"Zanna...what is that?"

"What?"

"That...*stuff* you were drinking. That *red* stuff."

"Oh, nothing important." Zanna took Dani's arm and started for the door.

"But it looked like..." Dani hesitated, suddenly very shaky inside.

If Zanna was the vampire, confronting her wouldn't be the smartest thing to do. But the idea of Zanna being the vampire was crazy. She was the last person in the world anyone would think...

More of Ion's words came drifting back. "Women are the most cunning of the Un-Dead." That was exactly what he'd said.

"What's the matter?" Zanna asked as they reached the dining room. "You're trembling."

"Ahh...nothing...I think I might have caught a bit of a chill, that's all."

"Oh, dear. Well you sit right down here beside me and I'll pour the tea. Something hot might help."

Dani let herself be settled in a chair, her mind whirling.

The vampire killings had slowed down. There'd only been one in the past week. And Karsten had told her that was strange, because when vampires went on binges, it usually took months of frequent killings to satiate their need for blood.

But maybe they could store it. Maybe in a nice cold place, like the castle's root cellar. Then have a drink of it whenever the craving struck.

The thought made Dani nauseous.

"There you go," Zanna said, passing her a cup of tea. "And you want biscuits, of course."

"No! No, nothing to eat. But..." She *had* to ask, because there *had* to be an explanation for what she'd seen—aside from the obvious one.

"Zanna, you've really got me curious. What was that stuff you were drinking?"

"Oh, just borscht."

"Borscht . . . as in beet soup? For breakfast?"

"No, no, silly. It wasn't breakfast. I was just tasting it. It's one of the recipes I've been practicing for Petre."

Dani tried to put a face to the name, but couldn't.

"You know . . . my betrothed? Petre Vaidescu? In Brasov?" Zanna eyed Dani curiously. "Are you sure you're not feeling *really* ill?"

"No, I'm fine." But her mind must have quit on her. Zanna had talked about her fiancé a thousand times in the past weeks.

"Didn't I tell you about his mother's recipes? I thought I did."

"Ahh . . . no. Tell me."

"Well, she sent me all of Petre's favorites by post, a month or so ago, so I could learn how to make them. I mean, I won't really have to *make* them after we're married, but I'll have to supervise our cook. So I've been trying them out whenever Tesia isn't using the kitchen. But the borscht has been giving me trouble. It keeps ending up too thick. And more blood-colored than wine-colored. I'm starting to think there's something wrong with the beets from our garden."

"Yes . . . yes, it did look like blood." But was that because it actually had been, or because there was something wrong with the beets from the castle's garden?

"Oh, by the way," Zanna said, "did Romulus find you?"

Dani drew another blank. Her mind really *had* quit on her.

"Earlier this morning," Zanna elaborated. "He arrived from the village a while ago. And before he and Sigismund and Ion started talking in the library, he was looking for you."

Of course. Romulus had been in the library with the others when she and Karsten had come over from the cottage. But that had been the first time she'd ever seen the man. "No, I guess he couldn't find me."

"Well that's strange. He said he wanted to talk to you, so I told him you were staying in the cottage. And that's where he was heading when he left me."

Dani bit at her lower lip uneasily. There was no way Romulus could have gotten lost between the castle and the cottage. The stand of pines wasn't *that* thick. But he certainly hadn't knocked on the door.

She tried to recall exactly what he'd said to her in the library earlier.

"I happened across some very interesting things," he'd told her. "And I'd like to talk to you about them."

Oh, heavens, what if the very interesting things he'd been referring to were things he'd *happened across* in her wardrobe? What if, like Ion before him, he'd used her bedroom window as a door?

DANI HESITATED at the castle entrance, glancing back across the foyer and down the corridor that led to the library.

If the vampire strategy meeting was still going on, she'd really like to catch the end of it. But Sigismund would have a fit if she tried. Besides, she had so many other things to think about that it might be better just to let Karsten fill her in.

"Well . . . bye," she said, turning to Zanna again.

Zanna wrapped her arms around Dani and gave her a long, hard hug.

Dani hugged her back, desperately not wanting her to be the vampire. And she probably wasn't. Surely if that *had* been blood, Zanna wouldn't have merrily turned the clean-up detail over to Tesia. So it *had* to have been borscht. Didn't it?

"Dani?" Zanna said, releasing her from the hug. "I really *am* certain I didn't say a single word I shouldn't have to Ion Dobrin. My brothers think I can't keep secrets, but I'm not quite as silly as they believe. I know when something's really important. And I can keep it to myself."

"Thank you," Dani murmured. "That makes me feel better."

She gave Zanna a goodbye smile, then started across the courtyard, gathering up her skirt so it didn't trip her on the cobblestones. They were the absolutely worst things to walk on in Danica Radulesco's slightly too-large shoes. Curling her toes under a little, she kept her eyes on the treacherous ground before her.

Zanna's words *had* made her feel better. Somewhat better, at least.

But even if Ion hadn't *heard* anything that would make him suspicious, there was still the worry that, standing outside her window, he'd *seen* something.

And if worrying about that wasn't enough, for a change of pace she could worry about that cryptic remark Romulus Teodescu had made. Were those *interesting things* he'd happened across items that had belonged to Danica Radulesco? Or had he meant—

"Danica?"

Her eyes flashed up from the cobblestones and she whirled around, almost losing a shoe in the process.

"Sorry," Romulus said, closing the distance between them with a few steps. "I didn't mean to scare you."

"It's all right. You didn't scare me. Just startled me a little." She glanced back toward the castle, hoping to see Karsten, but there was no one in the courtyard except her and Romulus.

"You're going to the cottage?" he asked.

Reluctantly, she nodded. She could hardly say she was going to the castle when she'd been heading away from it.

"I'll walk with you," he told her.

She managed a nervous smile, wishing she could walk faster in Danica's shoes.

The Nicholaes didn't like Romulus. And she knew Danica hadn't, either. There had to be reasons for that, but she doubted one of them was that Romulus was a dummy. He was reasonably well-spoken, and there was an intelligent look in his eyes—or perhaps *cunning* would be a better word.

Yes, she'd bet he was extremely cunning. And someone like that, if he was against you, could be very dangerous. Someone cunning might also be quick to realize that she was an impostor.

"I've been wondering," he said as they reached the pines, "if you've decided to come back to Castle Ceistra permanently."

"No," she said quickly. "No, I'll be returning to Walachia soon. I came only for a month, to visit Zanna."

"To visit *Zanna*," he repeated.

Dani nodded.

"I wondered ... when I saw you with Karsten...."

She forced another smile, instinct warning her to be careful what she said. "Karsten and Sigismund have *both* been very good about keeping an eye on me."

"Ahh ... so you and Karsten are not ... ?"

"No, of course not."

"That's good. Because I have a feeling there may be trouble in Karsten's future."

"Oh?" She tried to sound casual, but her pulse had begun to race. *She* had a feeling that whatever trouble was in Karsten's future, Romulus would be part of.

"If I were you, Danica, I wouldn't be spending too much time with Karsten Nicholae."

She nodded again, hoping she looked as if she appreciated Romulus's interest in her welfare. "As I said, both Karsten *and* Sigismund have been watching out for me. They've been worried about my safety. You may not have heard, but I had an encounter with the vampire a while back."

"Yes, I *did* hear. As mayor, I am told most things. And I just heard you saw him again last night."

For half a second, Dani wondered how he knew that. Then she realized that Ion and Karsten would have talked about it at the strategy meeting.

"Yes ... yes, I did. It was most frightening."

Romulus didn't speak for a minute. He simply walked along beside her, absently stroking his filthy beard.

She half expected that, any second, he was going to disturb something living in it.

"You know," he said at last, "if neither you nor your mother come back to Castle Ceistra, the Nicholaes will continue living in it."

"Yes, I guess they will. My mother intends to stay in Walachia, though. As do I."

"I see."

There was another long pause, and Dani prayed that the discussion was finished.

Her prayer wasn't answered, though, and Romulus continued. "I was thinking," he went on, "that we never had occasion to talk after your marriage. But I was sorry for all your trouble, Danica. Sorry to hear about your husband being killed."

"Thank you."

"And your brothers, of course...and your father."

"Yes," she murmured, certain she looked appropriately unhappy. Romulus was making her so uncomfortable she could hardly be looking anything but.

He suddenly turned in front of her and made a grab for her hands.

She stepped quickly away, hiding them behind her back, and gave him a nervous little shrug. "Romulus, please. It's not all that long since my husband was killed. And I'm just not...you know."

He looked extremely displeased, but nodded. "I understand. But, Danica, things have changed since your father said I wasn't good enough for you. I'm the mayor now. I'm highly respected by the people of the village."

"Yes, I'm sure you are."

"And a woman like you needs a man to protect her. If you come back permanently, take your rightful possession of the castle, I'll be able to provide that protection. You'd be both the mayor's wife and the mistress of the castle.''

And you, Dani thought, would get what Zanna once mentioned you wanted—Castle Ceistra.

"Well, Danica?"

"I...Romulus, I'm flattered. Very flattered. But as I said, I intend to stay in Walachia with my mother and—"

"Wait. Don't give me a final answer right now."

An anxious little shiver seized Dani. His tone wasn't *asking* her to wait. It was ordering her to.

"I'll give you a couple of days to think on this, Danica. Because you should consider what would happen if the villagers heard about those *interesting things* I mentioned earlier. Why, when a woman has things that mystify even a mayor, things that only a witch would have...what would people think if they saw things like these?" Romulus reached in his pocket and produced two of her credit cards.

"*You,*" she whispered. "Give those back to me. You had no right to take them."

"I'm the mayor. That gives me certain rights. And obligations. Danica, many of the villagers are still convinced that you've become a vampire. I was merely looking for proof—either way. But now that I've found these things, these instruments of witch-craft—"

"They're not instruments of witchcraft! That's ridiculous."

"Oh? Then what are they? And what strange substance are they made of?"

"They're...never mind what they are. This is none of your business."

"Oh, but it is. It's the *mayor's* business. And if I told my people there was a witch in their midst..."

"You wouldn't! You don't really believe I'm a witch!"

"That's as it may be. I certainly wouldn't say anything to make people think that if you decided to marry me. So you consider it for a couple of days. I'll be waiting to hear from you. If I don't..."

Romulus gave her an exaggerated shrug. Then, without another word, he slipped her credit cards into his pocket again and turned back toward the castle.

ONE LOOK AT DANI'S FACE told Karsten something was terribly wrong.

He glanced over at the closed bedroom door, then quietly said, "There's no one in there this time, is there?"

"No. And the window's tightly latched. But...oh, Karsten..."

He locked the front door, crossed to the couch and sank down beside her.

"Tell me," he said.

She didn't say a word, merely wrapped her arms around his neck and clung tightly.

He hugged her to his chest, her warm softness making him hard with desire. She smelled as wonderful as she always did—that indescribable scent that made him think of exotic places and hidden pleasures.

He didn't care much about the exotic places, but thinking about the hidden pleasures was driving him crazier and crazier. And knowing, from things she'd told him, that in her world they'd go right ahead and enjoy those pleasures... well, maybe he was an imbecile not just to go right ahead even though they *weren't* in her world.

But given the bizarre circumstances, he knew she couldn't decide what was right and what was wrong. And he didn't blame her for being confused. He just didn't know how much longer he could stand not making love to her.

"Oh, Karsten, I love you so much," she finally murmured. "But we're never, never going to make things work out."

"Sure we are." He brushed her forehead with a kiss. "You'll go home, but you'll come back to me as soon as you can. Next September, in less than a year. And everything will work out just fine."

"No, it won't. Nothing's going to be fine. Karsten, I can't come back. Not ever."

"Of course you can. You just—"

"No. I can't, because if I did, Romulus would tell people I was a witch. Karsten, it was Romulus who looked through my things, not Ion. And he stole two of my credit cards. And he says he'll show them to the villagers and tell them they're instruments of witchcraft unless..."

"Unless what?" Karsten asked, trying hard to control his anger.

"Unless I marry him."

"What?" The anger exploded, suddenly far too strong to be controlled. "Dammit, Dani, I'll kill him! I'll run him through before he can say a word to a single person."

"You can't! You can't go killing *anyone,* let alone the mayor. You'd end up being hung as a murderer."

"Well, I'll go talk to him, then. I'll make him see reason. I'll…dammit, Dani, I'll do whatever it takes."

"No, you don't understand. You wouldn't be able to make him see reason, because he wants Castle Ceistra. That's why he wants to marry me. So he'll get the castle."

"But he *won't* get the castle. We know that Sigismund will be living here years and years from now."

"But *Romulus* doesn't know that. Karsten, listen to me. Once I'm gone, once he's certain he won't be able to get the castle through me, he'll try to get rid of your family. And even though we know he won't ultimately get rid of Sigismund, we don't know about you."

"Dani, nothing's going to happen to me. How many times do I have to tell you that?"

"It doesn't matter how many times you tell me, because I *know* Romulus is going to cause you trouble and…oh, Karsten, you're liable to have both Ion *and* Romulus telling people you're the vampire. So you've *got* to come with me when I go. It's the only logical solution."

He held her tightly, letting everything she'd said sink in. Once she left, she could never come back, because Romulus would tell people she was a witch.

And that meant either going to the future with her or never seeing her again.

He couldn't leave with her. But how could he stay without her? His ribs seemed to be tightening around his heart like steel bands, making it almost impossible to breathe.

"Karsten?" Dani whispered, gazing at him. "Please say you'll go with me."

She began to trace his mouth with her fingers, driving him crazy with her touch.

"You're so beautiful," he whispered, "I can't even think of living without you, Dani."

Karsten's words sent such a surge of relief through Dani that she almost began to cry. But then he was covering her mouth with his and sliding her down beside him on the couch as he kissed her.

She wanted him so badly her body was aching, and feeling him hard against her only made that aching more intense. She moved her hands to his hips and pulled him closely to her.

He groaned her name, his tongue exploring her mouth and his hands moving to her breasts.

"Oh, Karsten," she murmured as he grazed her nipples. "Karsten, I want to make love to you here and in my world, too. I want to make love to you everywhere and forever."

She undid the buttons of his shirt and smoothed her palms across his chest, making him shiver at her touch.

Then he started kissing his way down her throat, fumbling at the buttons on her dress and kissing farther with each one he got undone.

"Hey," he murmured, pushing the front of her dress open and running his hands lightly over her sports bra. "This covers more of you than I'd imagined." He gave her a teasing smile, then lowered his head to her breasts.

Through the fabric, he kissed each hard nipple in turn, then began to caress them with his thumbs, driving her mad with need.

"It slides off at the shoulders," she whispered breathlessly.

He smiled and took the hint, then lowered his head again, catching one nipple in his mouth and teasing it with his tongue while he continued to caress the other with his thumb.

Dani moaned, burying her hands in his hair and moving her hips against him, trying to ease the throbbing ache inside her. But the more he kissed her, the stronger the ache grew.

His kisses trailed to her stomach and she arched her hips so he could slide her dress down over her legs.

"Now these," he whispered, slipping his fingers beneath the silk of her panties, "don't cover any more than I'd imagined at all."

She reached for him then, unable to wait a moment longer. But he was so hard she couldn't budge a single button on his fly.

"Oh, Lord," she groaned, "Karsten, how did people manage before zippers?"

Somehow, *he* managed, then urgently thrust inside her, murmuring how much he loved her.

DANI LAY SNUGGLED against Karsten on the couch, in the warm afterglow of their lovemaking, anxiously tangling his chest hair around her finger.

She had absolutely no idea what level of female sexual response was considered normal in 1850 Transylvania. But regardless of place and time, her orgasm had been so fast and violent it was almost embarrassing.

"Karsten?" she murmured against his chest.

"Mmm?"

"I... ahh, don't know quite how to put this, but that's never happened to me before... like that."

"No?" he said, eyeing her with a mile-wide grin.

"No. I mean, it only happened because you made me feel... I can't even begin to describe how you made me feel. But it was incredible and wonderful and fantastic and unbelievable, all at once."

"So... I measure up to men from the future, then?"

"Measure up?" She couldn't keep from laughing. "Karsten, I really haven't had that much experience with other men, but from what little I *have* had, I'd say you're in a whole different league."

"That's good?" he asked uncertainly.

"Good?" She nuzzled his chest. "*Good* is a major understatement. When you come to the future with me, we're going to keep this a deep dark secret. If we don't, I'll have to beat off other women with a stick."

He looked a little worried, so she gave him a quick kiss and said, "I'm joking, Karsten. About the stick, at least. But not about how you made me feel."

"I know. I mean, I realized you were joking. But... Dani, I never said... I never said that I'd go to the future with you."

An icy chill began creeping up her spine, and her nakedness suddenly made her feel vulnerable.

Reaching down to the floor for her dress, she pulled it over her like a blanket, saying, "But I thought... Karsten, you *did*. You said, 'I can't even think of living without you, Dani.' Those were your exact words."

He propped himself up on his elbow and cleared his throat.

That started a second icy chill creeping along after the first.

"I guess I *did* say that...and I *did* mean it...that I don't know how I'll even be able to think of living without you. And we've just made it worse yet to think about. But, Dani, I didn't mean I'll be able to leave with you."

She gazed at him, knowing that her eyes were pleading with him but not caring. She'd get down on her knees and beg if that's what it took. Because if he didn't go with her, her heart would break.

"Karsten, I love you. So don't say you *can't* leave, as if it were written in stone. Don't try to think about living without me. Think about coming with me. Because I really, really don't want to try to live without you."

"And I really, really don't want to try to live without you, either," he murmured. "But sometimes, there's just no way to get what you *do* want. No matter how badly you want it."

Chapter Twelve

Dani stared out into the darkness, unable to stop thinking that the past week had been the most miserable of her life. She'd lived through it in a state of numbness, only forcing her brain to work whenever a message arrived from Romulus Teodescu, pressing her for her decision.

In each response, she'd given him the best delaying tactic she could come up with. And while the tone of his letters had grown more and more impatient, he hadn't yet carried through on his threat. If he had, the villagers would have come to drag her off.

She shook her head, not wanting to think about Romulus *or* the villagers. And, most of all, she didn't want to think about Karsten.

But that was impossible, even though they'd been seeing no more of each other than they had to. Except for meals, which she'd mostly eaten alone in the castle kitchen, she'd been staying here in the cottage— while he had intentionally stayed away from it. From early every morning until late every evening, when he'd come in to take up his post on the couch.

That hadn't been nearly enough, though, to keep him from her thoughts. Falling in love with him, then discovering there was no possible happy ending for their love, was the worst thing she'd ever experienced.

She swallowed over the lump in her throat while her eyes, as they'd done so frequently of late, strayed to the moon.

Each night it had waxed a little fuller. Each night it had brought her closer to the time when she'd have to leave. And now she was only one day away. Tomorrow night was the night of the hunter's moon.

Tomorrow night she'd be gone. Without Karsten. Whatever the reason he felt he *had* to stay in his own time and place—the reason he'd steadfastly refused to share with her—it was obviously more important to him than she was.

She turned away from the window, almost not caring anymore what his reason was. Just as she almost didn't care any more who the vampire was.

The trap Ion Dobrin had laid hadn't worked. There'd been no sign of the vampire at all lately.

Not unless, of course, it had been walking around in mortal form, right under their noses. Maybe as Zanna? Sigismund? Maybe even Letcha, whom Ion Dobrin's dog instinctively disliked?

Of course, really believing Zanna was a vampire was impossible, despite the lingering image of her drinking that borscht . . . or blood. But even if the impossible were true, Zanna would be safe. She'd be the last suspect the villagers would ever get around to. And, come spring, she'd be married and off living in Brasov with her Petre Vaidescu.

As for Sigismund...well, Dani still didn't find it totally impossible to believe Sigismund might be the one. But even if he was, he wouldn't be caught. She knew he'd be living in Castle Ceistra for years and years to come.

And Letcha might make her uneasy, but neither that nor Lupus disliking him was hard evidence of vampirism. Besides, if the vampire wasn't a Nicholae, it could just as easily be someone she'd never even met. Any one of millions of people.

At this late date, she doubted she was ever going to learn the creature's mortal identity. But regardless of its *real* identity, she was still worried sick that people would eventually decide it was Karsten. She'd tried not to care about the possibility of that happening. In fact, she'd even tried to hate him. But she'd failed miserably. Because it was obvious that his decision to stay was causing him almost as much pain as it was her.

Czar nuzzled her hand and she absently stroked his head, saying, "I'll miss you when I go, fellow."

Her vision blurred. She *would* miss the dog, but she'd miss Karsten a thousand times more.

She wiped her eyes, gazing out into the night once more. Then she saw Karsten step out of the stand of pines and start across the moonlit clearing.

After tonight, she wouldn't be waiting here to let him in. Tomorrow night, she'd be back in her own world. A world without the man she loved.

The thought made her feel utterly empty. She could return to her time, but her heart would remain here.

Pulling her robe more securely around her, she unlocked the door.

"Hi," Karsten said, not meeting her eyes.

"Hi . . . anything new?"

He gave her a tight-lipped shrug that said he couldn't bear to talk to her any more than she could bear to talk to him. It simply hurt too much.

"Well . . . good night, Karsten." She turned and headed for the bedroom, Czar on her heels and tears in her eyes.

She climbed into bed and lay tossing and turning in the darkness, wondering if Karsten would stay in the cottage all night or go off on one of his nocturnal wanderings.

It was difficult to believe he was still doing that, but he was. A violent thunderstorm had wakened her a couple of nights ago. And when her curiosity had sent her creeping into the living room, sure enough, Sigismund had been lying there.

Until then, she'd assumed that knowing Romulus had the castle under surveillance had put a stop to Karsten's nighttime expeditions. She should have known better, though. Learning he was being watched had simply made him adjust his routine.

From Zanna, who sometimes sat at her bedroom window late into the night, Dani had learned that Karsten was now using a secret passage to slip away from the castle grounds. It was nothing more than a wide crack in the wall. But, apparently, only the Nicholaes were aware of it. And for all Dani knew, Karsten was using it most nights. Totally unobserved by Romulus's spies.

But what did he do out there?

She didn't know. All she knew was that he couldn't possibly be out playing vampire. Whatever his secret, she was certain it was nothing evil.

Beyond that, she simply didn't have any facts. He'd told her almost nothing. The only thing she did know...

"My having to stay here," he'd said once, "has to do with my going out at night."

But that wasn't much of a clue.

Unless...what if she learned *why* he went out at night? Maybe, if she knew that, she'd understand his reason for staying. And if she understood his reason, she might be able to convince him it wasn't as important as he thought.

The more she considered that, the more it seemed a viable possibility. If she had the facts to use in her argument, she could try, one more time, to convince him he should leave with her.

So she had to make a decision. She could simply leave and never see him again. Or she could try to find out where he went and what he did.

Her mind began racing. She had only tonight left. Why hadn't she thought of this idea sooner? And exactly what was it that Ion had told her, way back when? She forced his words to surface.

"Master Karsten frequently leaves the grounds at two o'clock in the morning," he'd said. "The time is apparently quite consistent."

She thought for a few more seconds, then rolled out of bed and took her waist pack from the bottom of the wardrobe.

Dumping its contents on the bed, she found her watch. She pressed the little button that illuminated its face and set the alarm for 1:00 a.m.

After putting the watch on and scooping everything else back into the pack, she dug out her own clothes from the wardrobe and changed out of her nightgown, into her jeans and sweater.

Logic said it would be safe enough to wear them in the middle of the night. Nobody had ever stopped Karsten when he went out, so nobody would stop her if she was right behind him.

And riding horseback in the darkness would be bad enough, without worrying about a long dress catching on branches. Or, she mentally added, without worrying about too-large riding boots if she had to do any walking.

She put her sneakers directly beside the bed, then took the revolver from the bedside table. But how was she going to carry it? She tried sticking it in her waist, the way Karsten often wore his.

That didn't feel safe. All she could think about was that, bouncing along on Gabriel, she was liable to shoot herself. So, instead, she tucked it into her waist pack.

Then she crawled back into bed, carefully sliding her left arm under the pillow, so that the blare of the alarm would be muffled.

Fully dressed and ready, she closed her eyes, her heart pounding in anticipation.

FOR A MOMENT, Dani didn't realize where the noise was coming from. Then she quickly slid her right hand beneath the pillow, clicked the alarm button on her watch and lay without breathing, certain Karsten would come rushing into the bedroom any second.

She'd forgotten just how very loud and insistent that alarm was.

The cottage, though, remained blessedly silent.

Czar snuffled her face, no doubt curious about what was happening.

"Go back to sleep," she whispered.

When he obediently flopped down onto the floor again, she swung her legs over the side of the bed, smoothed her clothes with her hands, then stealthily crept to the door.

Cracking it open, she scoped out the living room.

With the moon almost back to full once more, there was enough light to assure her that Karsten was the man asleep on her couch.

But would he stay through the night? Or would Sigismund replace him?

There was no way of knowing. But she only had this one night left here. Which meant that she *had* to try her plan tonight and just hope Karsten would go out.

And if Sigismund *was* coming tonight, she didn't want to cross paths with him. So she closed the door and hurried back over to where her sneakers were waiting. She tied the laces, strapped on her waist pack—heavier than usual with the weight of her revolver—then reluctantly took a warm cloak from the wardrobe and draped it over her arm.

Wearing cloaks required a little getting used to, and she'd rather have had the freedom of just her jeans and sweater. But October nights in the Carpathians had proved to be awfully cold.

After telling Czar, a second time, to go back to sleep, she unlatched the bedroom window. Hoisting herself through the opening, she landed softly on the ground outside, then wrapped the cloak around her shoulders and hurried across the clearing to the dark stand of pines. The moment she started through them the moonlight was banished by the boughs of the trees.

Immediately, she began wishing she had a flashlight. The creatures of the night were out in full force. And each time she heard a sound her heart skipped a beat.

But the sounds were quiet ones, she reassured herself, just the rustlings of small animals in the underbrush. If she heard a loud one, though, her heart would likely stop entirely.

She hadn't given this plan a lot of thought. Not nearly *enough* thought, she decided, hearing one of those louder noises.

What if there was something other than *small* animals out here? What if there was something hiding in these trees that was a threat to her? Maybe something that had *already* threatened her? A big, two-legged creature of the night, like the vampire?

By the time she reached the far side of the pines, she was certain she was crazy to have left the cottage.

Once she was back in the moonlight, though, things didn't seem so bad. She hurried across the courtyard, past the darkened castle, then along to the stable.

When she opened the door, the dogs began to bark, sending her heart into overdrive.

"It's all right," she called quietly into the darkness. "It's all right."

The kennel area was just to the left of the door, so she felt her way over toward it, still murmuring reassurances.

"It's okay," she whispered, sticking her hand between the boards. She'd never have dared do that if

Ion Dobrin's dog was in there, but all the borzois were as gentle as Czar.

One of them began licking her fingers, and they all gradually settled down.

"Good dogs. Good dogs," she told them, starting farther into the blackness.

Some of the horses snickered, but the sounds they made were quiet and comforting, and the smell of animals and fresh hay was reassuring.

She felt her way along the stalls, past Ebony's and on to Gabriel's. Murmuring quietly to reassure the horse, she unlatched the stall gate.

His bridle hung on the back wall and she managed to get it on him in the darkness. Luckily, after weeks of daily riding she felt comfortable enough to ride bareback. Saddling Gabriel in the dark would be a major challenge.

She'd scarcely finished with the bridle when she heard the stable door opening, with no prior warning from the dogs.

Heart pounding again, she sank down on her haunches in the hay.

A moment later, she heard Letcha's voice.

"What's the matter, fellows?" he asked softly. "What was all that noise about?"

Dani peered between two boards, but Gabriel's stall was so far along she could see nothing except a faint glow from Letcha's lantern.

Then he raised it above his head and started along between the stalls.

She shrank into a corner, trying not to even breathe.

He walked about halfway down the stable, stood listening for a minute, then turned and headed back to the dogs. He spent a good five minutes reassuring them, then finally left.

Dani let out a long, slow breath, surprised at his behavior. When he thought he was alone, he let his feelings show. Until tonight, she'd have bet he didn't have any. But she'd have been wrong. Letcha might not be good with people, but he was wonderful with animals.

Creeping up to the front of the stall, where she could see better, she sat wondering whether vampires had a reputation for being good with animals.

Finally, she turned her thoughts to how she should best follow Karsten without letting him see her. She'd just begun worrying that he wasn't actually going to go out tonight when the stable door opened again.

This time it was Karsten. He stood in the doorway for a moment, outlined by the moonlight, while he calmed the dogs. Then he started along between the stalls.

Dani scrunched down further, even though she was certain the dim light from the lantern he was carrying wouldn't reach as far as Gabriel's stall.

He spoke quietly to Ebony, quickly saddled him and led him out into the night.

The second he closed the stable door behind himself, Dani pressed the button that illuminated her watch face.

Quickly, she figured out how long a lead she could give Karsten without losing him. She shaved a minute off her estimate, for fear he might move faster than she expected, then led Gabriel out of the stable and started for that crack in the wall.

Sure enough, when they made it out of the castle grounds she could just see Karsten and Ebony in the distance. Without the moonlight, the night would have swallowed them. But, as things were, she could see them except when they hit a shadowy area.

Ebony was moving at a steady trot, so she started Gabriel after them, her throat dry and her palms damp.

Yet what was the worst Karsten would do if he looked back and saw her?

He'd get angry. But it wouldn't be the first time he'd been angry with her. Besides, he wasn't going to look back. He'd probably made this trip so many times that he never worried about being followed.

Dani trailed along just close enough to keep Karsten in sight, shivering a little in the cold night air.

He avoided the main road until he was more than a mile beyond the castle wall, then rode out onto it and started in the direction of Biertan Village. Was that where they were going?

It proved not to be. About half the distance to the village, Karsten turned Ebony to the left and disappeared up a narrow mountain path.

Dani gave Gabriel a little dig in the ribs, wondering whether she'd been hanging back too far. When she reached the turn she decided she definitely *had* been.

She couldn't see any sign of Karsten. In fact, the trail he'd taken was so overgrown and winding that it was impossible to see more than a few feet ahead. The dense, tangled growth blocked every beam of moonlight.

Giving Gabriel free rein to pick his way, she hoped for the best.

The trail grew steeper and slower, winding between trees and eventually following a sheer face of rock.

When it suddenly took a ninety-degree turn, Gabriel danced a little, negotiating it, then balked and came to an abrupt halt.

Directly in their path stood a tall man pointing a rifle at them.

Dani breathed in sharply, fear washing over her.

"I know who you is," the man said, "so don't try no tricks or I'll shoot."

"You... you know who I am?"

His nod was barely perceptible in the darkness. "You's the witch."

DANI SIMPLY COULDN'T quell her terror. Her heart was beating a mile a minute, and no matter how many deep breaths she took it refused to slow down.

Her captor hadn't spoken since announcing that he knew she was the witch. He'd simply bound her hands behind her back, tied Gabriel securely to a tree, then vanished.

When he'd reappeared, mounted on a horse of his own, he'd led Gabriel back to the main road and they'd started off down it.

This time, Dani suspected, she really *was* heading for Biertan Village.

"Where are you taking me?" she finally demanded.

"To the mayor."

The mayor. Romulus Teodescu. She was sorry she'd asked.

Fleetingly she thought about digging Gabriel in the ribs and trying to make a run for it. But galloping down the incline, with her hands tied and no saddle would be impossible. It was all she could do to keep from falling off at the pace they were going.

Besides, her captor was trotting along right beside her—both horses' reins in one hand and his rifle in the other.

Eventually they reached Biertan Village, rode past the enormous fortified church that dwarfed the little hamlet, then continued on down the main street.

The one and only time she'd been in the town before—in this century, at least—was the night she'd arrived in the past. And she hadn't really seen anything then. Karsten had simply hoisted her onto Ebony's back and they'd raced away.

Tonight, at this slower pace, she realized that the village looked almost the same as it did in the future.

She'd never seen it asleep and bathed in moonlight before, though. And she'd never before seen it with all the windows and doors festooned with garlic.

Aside from the moon, the only light was a faint glow coming from the Boar's Head Tavern, up ahead. And since she was being taken to the mayor, his tavern was undoubtedly their destination. It wasn't someplace she wanted to go at all.

The last time she'd been in that tavern, she'd almost ended up with a stake through her heart. And this time...

Well, she really didn't want to think about what might happen this time.

"You's the witch," her captor had said. So even though she was probably too frightened to be thinking straight, it wasn't tough to figure out that Romulus had finally made good on his threat. He'd told people she was a witch.

Sure enough, her silent companion reined in the horses when they reached the tavern, dismounted, and looped both sets of reins over a hitching rail. Then he motioned her down with his rifle.

She awkwardly slid off Gabriel, trying to keep her cloak from opening and revealing her clothes.

The man motioned again—this time indicating she should precede him into the tavern.

When she opened the door, stale, dank air rushed out at her. Given that her stomach was already churning, the combined aromas of smoke, ale and seldomwashed bodies almost made her vomit.

Choking back her nausea and fear, she stepped inside.

There were maybe twenty people in the tavern, all of them men. A hush fell over the room as they noticed her.

Leaning against the far wall, watching her, was Romulus. And the little man beside him, she realized, was Ion Dobrin.

Frightened as she was, she wondered what he was doing here in the middle of the night. He was supposed to be up at the castle, watching over the trap he'd laid for the vampire.

He'd explicitly told the Nicholaes that nobody could attend to the task except him—something to do with vampire hunters having a code of secrecy about their methods.

There wasn't much time to wonder about Ion, though, because her captor poked her in the back with the end of his rifle, telling the others, "I found her up to Castle Ceistra. Just outside the wall. She were lookin' fer the vampire. And she were talkin' to the moon.''

Hearing his words almost started Dani trembling. Things were bad enough without the man lying and making her sound crazy.

Then Romulus said, "Take off her cloak," and she stopped worrying about the lies and started worrying about what would happen when all these men saw her clothes.

A man behind her ripped her cloak away and the tavern was suddenly alive with voices.

"No mortal woman would ever wear breeches," someone shouted above the others. "That *proves* Danica Radulesco is a witch."

"Of course it does," Romulus agreed. "And what is that *thing?*" he demanded, pointing at her waist pack. "Is that what you use to carry your instruments of witchcraft?"

Somehow, Dani managed to dig up enough courage to glare at him through the smoky air. He knew what was in her pack. He'd already pawed through it.

"Take it off her," he ordered.

Rough hands tore at the strap and ripped the pack from her waist, almost knocking her to her knees in the process.

The man who ended up in possession of it carried it over to Romulus.

With an exaggerated motion, he pulled the zipper back and forth several times, demonstrating how the pack opened and closed.

The other men edged nearer, every bit as fascinated by the zipper as Karsten had been at first, but clearly frightened of it as well.

"Witchcraft," Romulus muttered loudly, pulling it open a final time. He reached inside the pack and removed her revolver.

That produced a round of muttering from the men.

Then he turned the pack upside down and dumped the remainder of its contents out onto the bar.

Gasps greeted the collection of makeup, safety pins, pens, Dani's driver's license, her little address book and the two credit cards Romulus hadn't taken his first time through her things.

"More witchcraft," he said firmly. "Tools of the devil, all of them."

"What should we do with her?" someone asked.

"Burn her," another man replied.

"Burn her! Burn her! Burn her!" Everyone seemed to take up the chant at once.

Dani looked to Romulus in utter panic. Surely he wouldn't allow this to proceed.

He held up one hand, silencing the crowd, giving her a glimmer of hope.

"I don't know if burning's the right thing for this one. Perhaps burying her alive would be better. In a secure, lead-lined coffin."

The glimmer died as quickly as it had been born. Being buried alive was a claustrophobic's worst nightmare. Even if she *was* only a marginal claustrophobic.

"What about her horse?" her captor asked, gesturing toward the half-open door with his rifle. "It's right outside there. Can I keep it when she's buried? I was the one what brung it here."

"Wait a minute!" someone snapped.

Through her terror, Dani realized it was Ion who'd spoken.

"All of you just wait a minute," he said. "Not long ago, you were convinced this lady was a vampire. Now you're certain she's a witch. But she lived among you from the time of her birth. Don't you think you'd have noticed, in all those years, if there was actually something so strange about her?"

"She's only become a witch since she left," Romulus said firmly.

"How can you be *sure* she's a witch?"

"Because she has those strange things." Romulus pointed at the items on the bar. "Witch's things."

"They aren't necessarily witch's things. I am an expert on these matters, and you can't be certain she's a witch unless someone has seen her practicing witchcraft. The strange things she has... there are explanations for strange things."

"What explanations?" someone demanded.

"You," Romulus snapped, glaring at Ion, "are an expert on vampires. Not witches."

Vaguely, Dani realized she'd progressed from trembling to shaking like a leaf. Romulus wanted these people to kill her. To burn her at the stake or bury her alive. And, aside from Ion, they seemed only too eager to cooperate.

"Listen to me," Ion shouted above the babble of voices that had started again. "Vampire hunters know about witches, too. And the thing to do is see if she can perform witchcraft or not. Untie her hands."

Everyone in Dani's field of vision looked at Romulus.

He shrugged. "Why not? But what witchcraft do you expect her to perform?"

"Let me think for a minute," Ion said as one of the men removed the rope from around Dani's wrists.

It had been cutting into them, so she stood rubbing them while she fearfully waited to hear what Ion decided.

"No, I know what's even better," he said at last. "We'll give her a test. That's what would be done at a proper witch trial."

While several of the men began murmuring their agreement, Dani tried to remember everything she'd ever heard about witch trials.

Wasn't a favorite *test* to throw the witch into a lake? Then, if she saved herself, it supposedly proved she was guilty—that the spirits of the water had rejected her because she was a witch. And the only way she could be deemed innocent was if she drowned—because that meant the spirits had accepted her as a mortal.

Talk about a no-win situation.

But maybe that wasn't what Ion had in mind, because there wasn't a lake nearby.

She eyed him, unsuccessfully trying to read his mind, then glanced at her things on the bar.

There wasn't a hope of reaching her revolver before somebody stopped her. And even if she could, there were twenty or so men here and only six bullets in the gun.

Nervously, she gave her wrists another rub, massaging where the skin around her watch had been chafed.

"What's the test?" someone demanded impatiently.

"Let me think on it," Ion snapped. "Just wait while I think on it."

IT SEEMED TO DANI that Ion's thinking had lasted an hour when he finally spoke again.

"To decide on the proper test," he announced at last, "I have to look at her teeth." He started over to her, the other men clearing a path for him.

"Open your mouth," he ordered, his bad breath almost flooring her.

She opened her mouth and didn't breathe while Ion peered at her teeth, checking them from several different angles.

"When we get to the door," he whispered, his mouth at her ear, "push me backward, then run like the wind to your horse."

Her heart began beating a mile a minute once more. This time because Ion was going to try and help her escape.

Oh, Lord, she was certainly never going to trust her first impressions again. How could she ever have thought he was a little ferret of a man? How could she have thought he was disgusting just because he had halitosis?

"Well?" Romulus demanded.

"The test we will use must be conducted outdoors," Ion said. "The witch should go first, with me. The rest of you follow."

He grabbed Dani's arm and started toward the half-open door. Over the pounding of her heart, she could hear the others falling in behind them.

As they neared the doorway, Ion loosened his grip so that he was barely holding her.

She took a final step, then whirled and shoved him backward into the men following them.

Then she sprinted toward Gabriel.

Tearing his reins from the hitching rail, she leapt onto his back. But just as she was wheeling him away from the rail someone grabbed her leg.

She lashed down with the end of the reins.

He ducked out of the way, then grabbed again, this time getting her foot.

Her sneaker came off in his hands and he fell backward, but he'd given the others all the time they needed.

They'd formed a wide circle around Gabriel.

Step by measured step, they began to close it.

Chapter Thirteen

Almost overwhelmed by panic, Dani watched the men of Biertan Village moving toward her. Step by threatening step they were closing the circle, leaving her no way out. No escape.

She tried desperately to think; Gabriel whinnied nervously, a sound almost as shrill as her alarm.

Her alarm. It was an insane idea, but she was in no position to reject anything simply for being insane.

Offering up a tiny prayer, she pulled out the *test alarm* button on her watch.

The sudden piercing blare stopped the men midstride.

"This is an instrument of witchcraft!" she shouted above the alarm's din, raising her arm straight up so they could see her watch. "Each one of you that I aim it at will die . . . a slow and horrible death."

The men glanced around uneasily, most of them looking in Romulus's direction.

"And you, mayor, will be the first to go!"

Romulus held his ground for a moment, making Dani terrified that he'd call her bluff, then he took a step backward.

As if that had opened floodgates, the men began stampeding back toward the tavern door, falling over one another in their haste.

Dani wheeled Gabriel around and dug her heels into his flanks.

He took off like a bolt of lightning, almost galloping through a man in his path.

They raced along the main street, past the old church and out of the village, Dani not glancing behind her even once.

Her revolver was still sitting on the bar of the Boar's Head. If anyone followed and caught her, she wouldn't have a chance. Her sole hope was to ride back to Castle Ceistra as fast as Gabriel could carry her.

The cold night air whipped at them, reminding her of that first night, when she'd ridden along this road at breakneck speed with Karsten.

The moon was bathing everything in its golden light, just as it had then. But tonight there was no Karsten. Tonight she had to save herself.

Finally, after the road began sloping upward into the mountains, she dared to look back.

All seemed quiet, so she pulled on Gabriel's reins, slowing him to a gentle trot before he grew winded.

"Good boy," she murmured, patting his neck. "Good boy."

Her heartbeat began to return to normal. If she could just get back to the safety of the castle, she wouldn't set foot out of the cottage again until it was time to leave forever. To leave forever, without Karsten, she silently added, her thoughts turning to him.

She'd failed tonight. She still didn't know where Karsten went or what he did. Still didn't know his reason for insisting he couldn't go with her.

So that was it. She'd done all she could but it hadn't been enough. And now she'd be going back alone to the time where she belonged. And she'd have to live the rest of her life without the man she loved.

Her cheeks grew wet with tears and she fiercely brushed them away. But she couldn't brush away her thoughts of him.

"Sometimes," she remembered him saying, "there's just no way to get what you want. No matter how badly you want it."

And she wasn't going to get what she wanted this time, even though she wanted it more than anything else in the world.

A large cloud passed slowly in front of the moon, gradually covering its entire face. As the night grew darker, she slowed Gabriel's pace even more.

The road curved, passing between a rock facing and a stand of trees. It was a spooky little stretch, as narrow and black as a tunnel, and it made the hairs on the back of her neck stand on end.

After what had already happened to her tonight, though, worrying about a narrow bit of road was absurd. She was right in the midst of telling herself that, when someone suddenly threw a blanket over her head and yanked her off Gabriel.

Her struggling proved useless. When she hit the ground, her assailant wrestled her down, pressing the blanket against her face and pinning her arms.

Gabriel whinnied. A second later the man swore and leapt off her.

Karsten! It was Karsten's voice.

He tore the blanket from her, yanked her to her feet, then grabbed her by the shoulders, storming, "What the hell did you think you were doing tonight?"

The cloud had begun passing away from the moon, and his fury was as visible as it was audible.

"What?" he barked.

"I . . . Karsten, I just wanted to . . ."

"Dammit, Dani! You wanted to get us both killed? Is that it?"

She wiped her eyes, trying not to cry but unable to stop her tears.

Karsten let out a string of oaths while he picked up the blanket—actually, his cloak.

"Your shoe," he finally muttered, noticing she was missing one. "I knocked off your shoe. It must be around here someplace."

"No, I lost it in Biertan Village. One of the men there . . ."

The way Karsten began shaking his head made her stop explaining.

He didn't ask her to go on, simply said, "Get back on Gabriel. We've got to get out of here before half the village shows up looking for you."

KARSTEN UNLOCKED the cottage door and shoved it open, still not having said a single word since they'd started for the castle.

Dani limped in awkwardly with only one sneaker on, then froze in fear at the click of a gun being cocked.

"Stop or you're dead," Sigismund growled in the darkness.

"It's me," Karsten said.

He quickly lit a lamp, revealing Sigismund half-sitting, half-lying on the couch. His revolver was aimed straight at Dani.

"What the hell's going on?" he demanded, lowering it.

"Your chicken flew the coop," Karsten snapped. "Terrific job of watching over her."

Dani turned and glared at him. She'd had enough of his temper. "Actually, it wasn't Sigismund I snuck out on. I left while *you* were still here."

Sigismund pushed himself up into a full sitting position and gave Dani a look of utter disgust. "You're still leaving tomorrow night?

"Thank heavens," he muttered when she nodded.

Czar was whining in the bedroom, so she ignored Sigismund's comment and limped over to free the dog. He gave her hand a quick nuzzle, then trotted to the front door.

By that time, Sigismund had his boots on. Not bothering with a goodbye, he let both himself and the dog out, then slammed the door.

"Well?" Karsten demanded.

Dani sank onto the couch, so strung out she couldn't possibly go even a single round with him.

"Well?" he said again.

"Oh, Karsten," she murmured, "is this how you want us to end things? Angry and fighting? I'm sorry I followed you. It was the wrong thing to do. But I..."

She paused, wiping her eyes. She hated crying, but that's all she seemed to be doing tonight.

"Dani?" Karsten said quietly. He sank onto the couch beside her, feeling like a complete blackguard. He'd been frantic with worry about her and it had come out as anger. She was right, though. This wasn't how he wanted them to end. He didn't want them to end at all, but there was no way to prevent that.

"Dani, you're right. I'm sorry I yelled at you. But you could have been killed. Why on earth did you follow me?"

"Because I love you," she whispered, staring at the floor. "Because I love you, and I still want you to come with me when I go."

He swallowed hard. If there was only some way he could.

"And I thought," she went on, "that if I could find out *why* you won't leave, then maybe I could finally convince you that it isn't really such an important reason. But a man just appeared out of nowhere and took me down to the village and..."

"And?" Karsten prompted gently. "What happened when you got there?"

Dani took a deep breath, then told him the entire story.

"Good God," he muttered when she'd finished. "You came so close to getting killed. But why did Ion Dobrin help you?"

"I don't know. But who was that man with the rifle? I was right behind you, so he must have let you past. Why did he take *me* prisoner? Why did he drag me down to the village?"

"He was a guard, posted to watch for outsiders. And you weren't *only* an outsider. Romulus had told all the villagers that you were a witch. So our guard reported in, then took off with you. But I didn't learn about it until—"

"Karsten, I don't understand what you're saying. *Your* guard? And he reported in to whom? And how did you learn about it at all?"

Karsten rubbed his jaw wearily. It was only fair that he explain. And it should be safe enough to tell her now. She was as good as gone.

"You can't leave the castle grounds again," he finally said.

"I know."

"If it's the last thing I do, I'll manage to keep you safe here until you leave."

She nodded miserably.

"All right. You promise not to try anything else crazy?"

She nodded once more.

"Then...then I guess I can tell you. I've been afraid to, in case someone, somehow, got it out of you. But I'll tell you now because I don't want you to leave thinking I don't love you. Not when I love you more than I ever thought it was possible to love anyone."

"You love me that much...but it's still not enough," she whispered.

The way her eyes had filled with tears almost broke his heart, but there was a lot more to consider than just the two of them.

"Dani, I was at a meeting tonight. That's what the man was standing guard over. And he reported in to the fellow we had posted at the door, so he'd be replaced when he took you to Romulus. But I wasn't told anything about it until the meeting ended. Then, I'd just started down to the village after you when you came along. In the darkness, though, I didn't realize it was you. So I jumped you because I thought you were someone who'd learned where the meeting was."

Dani shook her head. "Karsten, I'm still not getting much of this. What was the meeting for? Why all the secrecy?"

He leaned back, running his fingers through his hair and trying to decide how to simplify the story.

"Do you remember," he finally began, "that a long time ago, I asked you what you knew about the future of Transylvania?"

"Vaguely."

"It was right after you told me you were from the future. And you said you knew the Austrian occupation wouldn't end until 1867, but you didn't know any names. Not even the name of the leader who'll eventually secure our independence."

"Yes, I remember now."

"Well... I think it might be me."

She looked at him blankly.

"The leader who eventually works everything out for the country. I think it might be me. Dani, I'm the leader of a nationalist group. That's where I go at night. To meetings like tonight's, or to deal with various issues."

"I... yes, I read something in Danica Radulesco's diaries. Something about your working with an underground organization during the revolution... and your father and Sigismund both disapproved."

"They still do."

"But you're the leader. I didn't know...."

"Well, I am. And *that's* why I can't leave with you. Dani, I might have a critical part to play in history. Maybe, without me, Transylvania would never become a free country again."

"But... but you don't know that for sure. If you left, somebody would take your place. And maybe he—"

"And maybe not."

"But everything turns out fine. The Austrians eventually leave Transylvania and—"

"The way things stand now, Dani."

She shook her head. "I'm not getting your point."

"My point is that we don't know a thing about how time travel works. *You* don't even understand it, and you've actually traveled to a different century. All you know is you got here by reciting that spell. So we don't have any answers about what would happen if I suddenly disappeared from this world."

"Someone else would take over as leader. Your leaving wouldn't change history, Karsten."

"You don't *know* it wouldn't. Like I said, we don't know anything for sure."

Tears had begun trickling down Dani's cheeks. He pretended not to notice, resisting the impulse to wipe them away.

"Karsten...what if the Austrians find out about this organization...find out you're the leader?"

He shrugged. She knew what would happen. There was no point in saying it.

"Or...you still might be killed as the vampire."

"Dani, I've just got to take those chances. Maybe, in the preordained order of the universe, it's critical that I stay here. That I remain leader. Maybe my leaving would change things for the worse. Maybe the eventual freedom of my country depends on my staying."

"So many maybes."

"I know. But I can't risk leaving in case they're facts."

"Not even though your staying means we'll never see each other again," Dani whispered.

"Not even though it does," he forced himself to say.

DANI WOKE ON THE COUCH, in Karsten's arms. They'd talked in circles until after dawn, until she'd been too exhausted to move even as far as the bedroom.

But they'd come up with no magic solution. None existed. Tonight, the hunter's moon would rise and she would leave.

She couldn't stay and Karsten couldn't go. The irresistible force and the immovable object. And finally accepting that had started a hollow aching inside her that she knew would remain as long as she lived.

When she tried to move without waking him, he opened his eyes and smiled sleepily at her. That made her feel worse yet, so she quickly slid along to the far end of the couch. The closer she was to him, the more desperately she wanted the impossible.

If she didn't have to wait until night, if she could leave right this minute, she would. Because the actual leaving couldn't be worse than being with him and knowing how soon she'd be without him.

For a moment, he looked as if he was going to reach out and pull her back to him. He didn't though. He had to realize, as well as she did, that every touch, every glance, every second together, was only making things harder on both of them.

"I'm starved," was all he finally said. "Let's go get some breakfast."

"You go ahead. I'd better change out of these jeans." There probably wasn't much point in trying to maintain her facade now that half the village had seen her in her own clothes. But she'd rather not have the servants gawking at her.

Karsten shoved himself up off the couch, then hesitated. "Dani, when you go back, what are you going to do?"

"Do?"

"About a job. You said a long time ago that your boss would figure you'd just deserted your group. So you'll be out of work."

"I'll find something. I . . . why are you asking?"

"I . . . I guess I was thinking in my sleep. Thinking that if we could somehow convince people here that you're not really a witch, after all . . . and if you don't even have a job to go back to . . ."

She slowly shook her head. "Karsten, last night I told twenty men that my watch was an instrument of witchcraft. I threatened them with a slow and horrible death. Can you imagine convincing them I'm not really a witch after that? Besides, there are still my parents to consider. I have to go. We both know that. And maybe . . ."

Searching for a way to change the subject, she picked up on his original question. "Maybe, when I get home, I could start my own tour company. Offer the sort of specialized trips that Living History Tours does. There's enough demand to support competition. And I know the business. All I'd need would be a bank loan or something to get started and . . . Karsten, what if I could really do that? What if I actually *could* get the money together and . . . I'd need guides. People who speak different languages. And you're so good at . . ."

Her words trailed off. They'd settled this once and for all last night. But here they were, both still grasping at straws, even though they knew there was no possible way they could end up in the same time.

"Just a minute," Karsten said. He headed into the bedroom and reappeared a few moments later with Danica Radulesco's jewelry case.

"These would get you all the money you'd need," he said, opening it. "Take them with you."

Dani gazed at the glittering collection of necklaces and pins, then shook her head. "They're not mine."

"No? Well whose are they? You're Danica's descendent. And we know that she never comes back to Castle Ceistra. So I'll bet my brother ends up keeping these things. In fact, I'll bet he ends up keeping the pieces Danica's mother left behind, as well. But they should rightfully belong to her heirs.

"Think about it," he added, putting the case down on the couch beside her. "And I'll see you at the castle in a few minutes."

"Yes, a few minutes is all I'll be." But after Karsten left the cottage she simply sat looking at the jewelry. He had a point. She could sell some of those pieces, or maybe she could even keep them in the family, simply use them as loan collateral.

Taking them with her would certainly make her life easier. At the moment, though, her life seemed so bleak that she didn't even want to think about it.

Forcing herself into motion, she put the jewelry case back in the wardrobe, then changed into one of Danica's dresses. She was just about to leave for the castle when someone knocked on the door.

She glanced nervously over at it, realizing she hadn't locked it after Karsten left.

Quickly, she took a rifle down from the gun rack. Zanna always called out a greeting, and Sigismund certainly never dropped by for friendly chats.

Leveling the rifle at the door, she called, "Come in."

Chapter Fourteen

"Oh, my." Ion Dobrin stood in the doorway, his vampire hunting dog at his side, and stared at the business end of Dani's rifle. "Oh, my dear lady, I mean you no harm."

"No, no, of course you don't," she said, quickly lowering the rifle. "And I'm so glad to see you. I want to thank you for helping me last night. If you hadn't, I'd be dead for sure."

Ion gave a self-deprecatory shrug. "I have a strong sense of right and wrong. What was about to happen in the village was wrong."

"Well, I can't tell you how much I appreciate what you did."

She glanced down at Lupus, then back at Ion, realizing this could be her last chance to talk to him.

"Mr. Dobrin, may I confide in you?"

"Of course."

"I . . . you probably haven't noticed, but I'm very fond of Karsten."

The hint of a smile appeared on Ion's face. "Actually, I *have* noticed."

"Ahh . . . well, the thing is that I'm terribly worried about what might happen to him. You . . . you *do* know by now that he isn't the vampire."

"I do not like to rule out *any* suspects too quickly, dear lady."

"But—"

"And I have a rule about not discussing my investigations until they are completed."

Her throat tight, Dani desperately tried to think of a way to convince him that Karsten was innocent. No brilliant ideas came to her. In fact, no ideas came at all.

"As I told you, though," Ion continued, "I do have a strong sense of right and wrong. So I'm very careful not to make a mistake. That is why I proceed deliberately."

Dani nodded unhappily. That was *something*, at least. He wasn't going to proclaim anyone the vampire until he was sure of his conclusion. But what if Ion *was* sure and . . . oh, what if he *did* make a mistake?

"There is something I must tell you," he said. "I came to warn you that the danger is not over for you."

"Oh?" Her worries about Karsten were joined by fresh ones about her own safety. What might still happen to her?

She only had to make it through the day, only until the moon rose tonight. But *only* was sometimes a very big word.

"You must leave Castle Ceistra, dear lady. You must not remain anywhere near Biertan Village. You shamed the mayor last night, by escaping, and he is already rousing the villagers to seek revenge."

"I *am* leaving. Tonight."

"Ahh, good. As long as you do, everything will be fine."

"You think I'll be all right here until nightfall, then?"

"I believe I can assure you of that. I shall be leaving for the village as soon as we finish speaking, to meet with Romulus Teodescu. I must talk to him about my conclusions and—"

"You have conclusions? You *have* decided who the vampire is!" Dani held her breath, but Ion merely shook his head.

"I should have said hypotheses, not conclusions. I have a theory I must discuss with the mayor."

"But you just said you have a rule about not discussing your investigations until they're complete. And you've got to have realized that Romulus isn't exactly—"

Ion held up his hand to silence her. "My dear, trust me. It was Romulus who sent for me, remember? He is my client. And, in this particular case, I feel I must discuss my theory with him."

"But..." Dani paused in frustration, not knowing what to say. Romulus hated both her and Karsten. Whatever trouble he could cause either of them he would. And heaven only knew what he'd tell Ion.

"As I was saying," Ion went on, "if you *do* leave tonight you'll be perfectly safe. I can promise you that no one will try to harm you today. While I'm speaking to Romulus, I'll advise him to tell his villagers to wait a day or two before they come after you."

"And you think he'll listen to you?"

"I'm *positive* he'll listen. After all, I spoke the truth last night. Vampire hunters *do* know about witches. And I know that you," he added quietly, "are not a witch. Despite the excitement you created with that strange watch you have."

Dani smiled uneasily. The vampire hunter had saved her life. And he'd just finished telling her that he'd ensure her safety today. So she likely had nothing to fear from Ion, but how did he know the truth? And how much of it did he know?

"You wonder how I know so much, don't you?"

She nodded, feeling even more anxious. Was the little man a mind reader?

"I have been blessed with certain powers," he explained. "They are of great help in my line of work. Sensibilities, some people call them."

"You're ...*psychic,*" Dani said, using the English word when Székely failed her.

Ion looked at her curiously.

"That's what we call it in ... where I come from."

"I see. And just where is it that you *do* come from? I know you are not the woman you pretend to be."

Her anxiety level inched up yet another notch. "I ... ahh, I actually come from quite far away."

"Yes, I guessed as much. But if you would tell me more, I would be most grateful. I sense you could add immensely to my knowledge of the extraordinary."

She managed another uneasy smile. Psychic or not, she doubted Ion had the faintest idea just how extraordinary her story was. But how could she not tell him what he wanted to know when she owed him her life?

"Well, Mr. Dobrin, why don't you come and sit down? This will take some time."

KARSTEN STRODE RAPIDLY across the clearing to the cottage, swearing at himself for leaving Dani alone.

She'd said she'd be right behind him. "A few minutes," she'd told him. But she still hadn't arrived by the time he'd finished breakfast.

Damn, if anything had happened to her . . .

"Dani?" he called, reaching the door and shoving it open.

"We're right here, Karsten."

He stopped dead. "What's going on?"

She was sitting on the couch with Ion Dobrin, his dog curled up asleep at his feet.

Dani looked perfectly fine. And the vampire hunter was wearing an expression of utter enthrallment.

"Mr. Dobrin was curious about where I was from. And not because he ever *saw* anything," she added pointedly. "He says I noticed him the moment he looked through my window that morning."

Karsten nodded. That might or might not be true. It didn't make much difference now, though.

"Anyway, I've just been telling him about home . . . and about how I got here."

"Oh?" Karsten glanced a question at her. Was she actually saying what he thought she was?

When she nodded, he exhaled slowly, not at all sure that telling Ion had been a good idea. But it was too late to worry about it.

"Positively amazing," Ion murmured. "Positively amazing. And when the hunter's moon rises tonight, dear lady, you'll go to the library and recite that spell? And then you'll simply disappear from 1850?"

"That's what I expect will happen. That's the way it worked coming here. I simply disappeared from the future and appeared here."

"Positively amazing," Ion murmured again. "I would very much like to see that. I had no idea your method of leaving would be so fascinating. But, my dear lady, now that you have confided in me, I feel I must confide in you. I did something that has been bothering me and I want to tell you."

"Yes?"

"That first night I spent at Castle Ceistra...the night the vampire appeared in your room?"

Dani nodded.

"Mistress Dani...there was no vampire in your room. It was simply me."

"What?" she whispered.

"What?" Karsten demanded, taking an angry step forward.

"Wait," Ion said, quickly holding up his hand. "Let me explain. What you saw *might* have been a vampire. The mist, the noise, it was all very accurate. A vampire most commonly enters a room in the form of mist. Traveling as a bat is..." Ion waved his hand dismissively. "None of the more *cosmopolitan* vampires would ever appear as a bat.

"In any case, your visitor was merely me, *replicating* a visit. The animal noises were noises I made. With help from Lupus. And the mist—smoke, actually—is a trick I have perfected over the years. I am quite an accomplished magician," he added with a trace of pride.

"But...but why?" Dani said. "You frightened me half to death."

"And I'm sincerely sorry that I did. Frightening the innocent is not a favorite part of my work. But it is a trick that has often served me well. If people are frightened enough, they usually tell me things they intended to keep secret. That is why I came to talk to you first thing the next morning. To hear your secrets."

"I . . . I didn't tell you any."

Ion smiled. "No. And now that I've heard the truth about you, I suspect I know why. In the future, people must have become too worldly wise for such tricks to work as well. But you do forgive me, do you not?"

Dani hesitated, finally giving him a reluctant "yes," while Karsten continued to glare at him.

But curiosity was mingling with his anger over the little man's trick. Despite all his earlier "positively amazings," Ion's reaction to discovering that Dani was from the future seemed very peculiar.

It had taken her hours to convince Karsten of the truth. The same with Zanna and Sigismund. But Ion seemed to have simply accepted the fact.

"Mr. Dobrin," he said, "You're making me wonder about something."

"Yes?"

"Well, I found the whole idea of time travel awfully difficult to believe. Yet you don't seem to have the slightest doubt that it's possible."

"No . . . no, that's because it fits with something I'd already sensed. I was sure that the young lady was going to vanish tonight. I almost," he added, looking at Dani, "didn't bother coming to warn you about leaving. Because my belief that you would be going was so strong."

He turned back to Karsten. "But, you see, the feeling I had was that she'd disappear without a trace. In a most mysterious way. I couldn't imagine exactly what the way was, but this explains it."

"Mr. Dobrin is psychic," Dani offered.

"He senses things most people don't," she explained when Karsten shot her another questioning glance. "That's what makes him so good at identifying vampires. At any rate, he sensed that I wasn't really Danica. And that I wasn't from around here."

Karsten nodded, absently thinking that saying she wasn't from around here was a great example of what she called *understatement.* "So," she went on, turning back to Ion, "have I answered all your questions yet?"

He slowly shook his head. "I *do* wish you knew more about how this time traveling actually works."

"I do, too. In fact, Karsten and I were saying exactly that last night. We have no idea how people's moving around in time affects the future...but wait."

Karsten looked at Dani again. The excitement he'd just heard in her voice was also on her face.

"Back up for a minute, Mr. Dobrin," she went on. "Something you said...that you *sensed* I was going to vanish tonight. You can...can you foresee the future?"

"Oh, yes. I frequently have premonitions. And, if I concentrate hard enough, I can see into the future for many, many years."

"How many?" she asked, her voice barely audible.

"Oh...twenty...thirty. I suspect it's until the end of my lifetime."

Dani simply sat staring at Ion Dobrin for a minute, then she looked at Karsten.

He knew exactly what she was thinking and his heart began to pound. If he could be certain that his leaving wouldn't jeopardize his country's fight for freedom, he'd go with her in a second.

"Mr. Dobrin," Dani said, her voice still not at its normal level. "Now that I've told you my story, I'd like to ask you about something."

"Of course, dear lady."

"Wait!" Karsten said, suddenly realizing the danger that lay in this.

Dani glanced at him uncertainly.

Ion looked curious.

"Excuse us . . . just for a minute." Karsten grabbed Dani by the arm and hustled her into the bedroom.

"You can't ask him," he whispered the instant he'd closed the door.

"What do you mean, I can't ask him? I've just answered ten thousand of his questions. He'll feel obliged to answer a couple of mine."

"That's not the point. Dani, if you ask him whether I'm going to be important in freeing us from Austrian occupation, he'll realize I'm involved in the movement. And I don't know that we can trust him. He might go straight to the Austrians and tell them about me."

"Oh, Lord, he might at that," she murmured. "And he's going down to the village later. To talk to Romulus. And if he said anything that Romulus could use against you . . ."

"Exactly. So you *can't* ask him."

"I . . . all right. We won't ask about *you*. But, Karsten, this might be a miraculous chance for us. We can't just let it pass by. At least let's see if we can find out anything useful."

Karsten ran his fingers through his hair, half wanting to try, half-afraid that Ion would know exactly what they were really asking. The little man was far more clever than he'd initially appeared.

But if there was any chance at all...Dani was right, they couldn't just let it pass by. Because then the only possible ending for them was that she'd be gone and he'd still be here. The only woman he'd ever loved would vanish from his life forever.

"All right," he finally said. "But we've got to be damn careful what we say."

They trailed back into the living room and Dani took her seat on the couch once more.

Karsten leaned against the fireplace, trying to look casual, while his heart was thudding so loudly that people could probably hear it in the castle.

"I apologize for the interruption," Dani said to Ion. "We just...well, that's not important. But what I wanted to ask you about has to do with the future."

"Oh, my dear lady, *you* want to ask *me* about it? You must know a million times more about the future than I could ever hope to."

"Well...yes. About the distant future. But what I was curious about was something closer to now. You see, I've told Karsten stories about what will happen in Transylvania over the next decade or two. Things I remember my grandmother telling me."

Ion nodded.

"And he was surprised that the Austrian occupation is going to continue for so long. Until 1867."

"Until seventeen years from now," Ion said.

Both his face and his voice were expressionless. Karsten had no idea whether Dani had told the little man something he'd already foreseen or not.

"And the more we talked about it," she continued, "the more curious we became. You see, I can't remember any names of the people who assure that the country finally does regain its independence."

"And I keep wondering," Karsten added, even though he suspected he might be pushing things too far, "if anyone I know plays a part in it."

"So I was thinking that maybe you could tell us," Dani said, giving Ion a big smile. "Satisfy our curiosity."

"Ahh," he said. "Ahh... well, I would like to do that, but I'm afraid I can't."

"You don't know," Karsten said, Ion's words dashing his hopes. So much for them being given a miraculous chance. Ion had just slammed the door on that possibility.

Ion scratched at the carbuncle on the side of his nose for a moment, then said, "It's not that I don't know, Master Karsten. If I put my mind to it, I imagine names would come to me. But when Mistress Dani said she wanted to ask me about something, it didn't occur to me that...well, I didn't realize she'd want me to play fortune-teller. That's something I never do."

Dani gave Karsten an anxious glance, then looked back at Ion. "Never?"

"No. You see, someone wise once said that the veil hiding the future was woven by angels of mercy. And I am not so foolhardy as to interfere with the work of angels."

He looked from Karsten to Dani, then back. "I'm sorry," he said quietly. "I can see that disappoints you, but..."

Ion paused, checking his pocket watch, then pushed himself up off the couch. "I must leave or I will be late for my meeting with Romulus. And I may not see you again, my dear lady, so I'll wish you a safe trip home."

"Thank you," Dani whispered as the little man turned to go.

Karsten followed him over to the door and locked it after he'd left. Then he looked back at Dani, his chest tight and his throat aching.

She gazed across the living room at him, her eyes glistening, but didn't say a word.

He knew she wouldn't ask him again. She understood how important it was that he remain. And yet, looking at her, it was all he could do to stand the thought of staying while she left, of living the rest of his life without her.

If only he were certain he'd really be needed here in the years to come. Being sure of that, it would be easier to convince himself the sacrifice was worth the pain.

"You know," Dani finally murmured, "once I'm home, I'll be able to find out what happens. That seems so strange, but somewhere, in a library or an archive, there'll be a detailed history about Transylvania gaining its freedom. And it will name the men involved. If I want to, I'll be able to check, Karsten. And see what part you played."

"And will you?"

She gazed at him without replying.

"Will you check? Find out whether I played an essential part or not?"

"I don't know," she whispered, a tear trickling down her cheek. "If I learned that your coming with me wouldn't have made any difference to history, I don't think I could bear it."

Chapter Fifteen

Her little entourage stopped in front of the library door, and Dani took a deep breath. The month that had stretched before her like an eternity when she'd first arrived had flown by in the blink of an eye.

She looked at Zanna, then Sigismund, trying to smile. She didn't risk even a glance at Karsten, though. Throat tight, eyes burning, she was barely managing to hold back her tears. And the moment she looked at him she'd be done.

"Oh, Dani," Zanna said, giving her a hard hug. "I'm going to miss you so much. You won't be here for my wedding. And I'll never see you again and—"

"Shh, Zanna. I'll miss you, too. But you're forgetting that I'm not really Danica Radulesco. You can see *her* again. Have Petre take you to Walachia and visit her. I know she'd be thrilled if you did."

Zanna wiped her eyes, then nodded firmly. "You know, I'm going to do that. Just as soon as I can after the wedding. And I'll tell her all about you and your family. She'll be so proud to hear that her descendents prospered and went to the new world. To Cal..."

"California," Dani supplied, imagining Zanna trying to convince Danica Radulesco that one of her descendents had come visiting from a hundred and fifty years in the future.

Sigismund cleared his throat and she looked at him once more.

"I wish you a safe voyage, Dani. I truly do."

That was the kindest thing he'd ever said to her, and it made her throat tighter yet. "Thank you, Sigismund," she managed. "And thank you for spending all those nights on my couch, looking out for me."

He gave her a curt nod and Zanna took his arm. "Let's go, Sigismund. Karsten will see her off. Bye, Dani. I really *will* miss you."

"Bye Zanna . . . Sigismund." Dani watched them start back down the hall. Neither of them could be the vampire. Looking at them, she was as certain of that as she was of her own name.

She waited until they'd disappeared into the entrance hall, then finally turned to Karsten, blinking fiercely to keep her tears at bay for a little longer.

His mouth was a thin line and he looked more unhappy than she'd have thought possible.

Without a word, he reached out and opened the library door.

She forced herself to step into the room, then stood gazing across to the desk.

Someone, Karsten, she imagined, had put the book of spells on it, and the crystal paperweight was holding it open at what she knew would be the right page.

Outside, the hunter's moon was beginning to rise; moonbeams were reaching into the room, dancing sparkles on the crystal.

"Mistress Radulesco?" a man said.

Startled, Dani looked around.

"I'm outside," he said.

Her eyes flashed to the window. Outside stood Letcha. He was wrapped in a dark cloak, only his face visible. And in the moonlight, it looked as pale as a ghost's...or a vampire's.

Dani's pulse began to race. Was Letcha the one, after all? And had he come, at the last moment, to keep her from escaping safely?

He beckoned to her with one long finger. Were his hands really as white and bony as a skeleton's? Or had her imagination geared into overdrive?

She glanced at Karsten. He didn't seem the least bit alarmed, so she uneasily moved closer to the window.

"I heard you was leaving tonight," Letcha said.

Dani nodded.

"Well, I..." he paused, looking awkward. "I just wanted to say that I know how much you come to like Czar. So I just wanted to say that I always take good care of the dogs."

That did it. Her tears spilled over.

She knew she couldn't take Czar back to San Diego with her. And even if she could, he was far better off here, where he had other dogs for company and rabbit chasing for fun. But knowing that hadn't kept her from crying when she'd hugged him goodbye in the cottage. And now...

She wiped at her tears and swallowed hard. "I know you take good care of the dogs, Letcha," she finally managed to say. "*Excellent* care. But thank you for reminding me. I'll remember that whenever I miss him."

"Uh-huh," Letcha grunted, then turned and started away through the moonlight.

"He *is* a strange one," Karsten said quietly.

Dani nodded. Letcha was strange. But not the vampire. She had the same feeling that she'd had watching Zanna and Sigismund walk away. It didn't look as if she'd ever have the answer to the riddle.

Then she looked at Karsten again and forgot all about the vampire riddle. Because there was something so very, very much more important that she was never going to have.

She turned away from him, taking off her cloak and draping it over a chair, trying to gain even a little control.

Karsten stood gazing at Dani. She was ready to leave, dressed in her own clothes. Except for the pair of Danica's shoes she had to wear because she'd lost one of her own. Lost it when the villagers had attacked her, thinking she was a witch.

If not for their believing that, she might be intending to come back to him. But the way things were, she never could.

When she turned to face him, her cheeks were damp with tears.

He swallowed hard, not certain he could get through this without tears of his own...not certain he could get through this at all.

He wanted to go with her so badly that he wasn't sure his patriotism was strong enough to keep him here.

Looking away from her, he opened the leather bag he'd been carrying over his shoulder. "I brought a couple of things for you to take with you. I...I don't know whether you'll want this...but my mother hired an artist to paint all the family members a couple of years ago."

He handed her the little portrait of himself that he'd taken from his mother's room.

"Oh, Karsten," she murmured, her eyes luminous. "Of course I want it. I'll treasure it . . . always. I wish I had something to give you, but . . . no, wait."

Slipping off the intricate gold ring she always wore, she placed it in his hand. "It's too small for you, I know. But it's all I have that means anything to me. It was my grandmother's, then my mother's. She gave it to me on my twenty-first birthday."

He merely nodded, not certain he could speak, but he'd put the ring on a leather thong around his neck and never take it off.

Dani stood looking at his portrait, and he could tell he wasn't the only one fighting to master emotions.

Finally, he cleared his throat and went on. "While you were saying goodbye to Czar, I checked the wardrobe and saw you'd forgotten this." He took Danica Radulesco's jewel case from the bag and held it out.

"I . . . Karsten, I didn't forget it. I just don't feel right about taking her jewelry."

"Take it. Here, I'll put everything back in the bag for you. Give me the portrait."

She silently handed it back to him and he put it in with the jewel case again, then placed the bag on the floor beside her.

"Dani, don't feel funny about taking those pieces. They belong to Danica's descendents. And they'll give you the means to start your business. They'll give you a good future."

"Oh, Karsten," she cried, tears suddenly streaming down her face. "I *can't* have a good future. Not without you." She threw herself into his arms and stood sobbing against his chest.

His cheeks wet with his own tears, he held her close and stroked her hair, breathing in her scent for the last time. The indescribable scent that made him think of exotic places and hidden pleasures...pleasures he'd never know again.

"You *will* have a good future," he insisted, forcing the words past the lump in his throat. "Eventually, you'll forget all about me."

"No I won't. I'll never forget you. Not if I live to be a million."

"Oh, Dani...this has all been so incredible that...after a while, it's going to start seeming like a dream to you."

And it would someday seem like a dream to him, as well. Sooner or later, once the pain had subsided some, he'd stop believing a woman could possibly have felt so good in his arms. Could possibly have made him so happy, simply by being with him.

"Karsten?" she whispered. "Karsten, I promised myself I wouldn't ask again but I can't help it. *Please* come with me?"

He took a deep breath and closed his eyes, then made himself say, "I can't."

HE'D HELD HER for as long as he dared, wishing he could hold her forever. But the spell specified light from the *rising* hunter's moon, and it was already well above the horizon.

"Dani?" he whispered, both his throat and heart aching. "Dani, it's time for you to go."

She pressed her body even closer to his and wrapped her arms around his neck, drawing his mouth to hers.

When he kissed her he could taste her tears...both their tears. He tried to kiss her tenderly but couldn't.

He wanted to devour her, to possess her, to make her his for all time.

But his time and her time were in two different centuries. And that made possessing her impossible.

Finally, he had to stop kissing her. If he didn't, he'd never be able to let her go.

When he drew his lips from hers she clung to him. He could feel her silently sobbing, and his heart felt as if it were about to break.

"Dani?" he forced himself to murmur. "Dani, try to stop crying. You have to read the spell."

She nodded against his chest, then edged away a little and wiped her eyes, not looking at him.

"All right," she whispered at last. "I'm ready."

"Don't forget this." He picked up the bag from the floor and passed it to her.

Through blurred vision, Dani gazed at it for a moment, making her decision. Then she opened the bag, took out the jewel case, and put it on the desk. "*You* keep the jewelry," she told him, carefully shrugging the bag with his portrait onto her shoulder. "You might need money to help with the movement."

He hesitated for a moment, then nodded. And without another word, he handed her the open book and the crystal.

Staring at the print, she couldn't get a single word to focus. She so desperately didn't want to go. Never in her life had she wanted anything more than she wanted to remain with Karsten.

But if she stayed she'd be killed. Sooner or later, Romulus would make sure of that.

Wiping her eyes again, she marshaled every bit of resolve she possessed, then concentrated on angling

the crystal so that it caught the moonbeams and reflected them back toward the window.

The words in the book still looked blurred, but she
could make out most of them now. Her throat aching, she began to read the spell.

She didn't look up from the book until she'd
reached the final line. Then, knowing it was a mistake, she glanced one last time at Karsten.

His face was wet with tears, and seeing that started
her own tears flowing again. But she'd already read the
last few words to herself.

Still looking at him, she whispered them aloud.

"Goodbye, Dani," he murmured. "I'll love you
forever."

Behind him, a mist suddenly began to swirl through
the window.

She started to point to it. Then she felt a tiny jolt
and Karsten was gone.

The moonlight was still streaming in through the
window, but the mist she'd seen had vanished, as well.

Uncertainly, she looked around. The book and
crystal were no longer in her hands. They were sitting
on the surface of the desk once more.

The library seemed brighter, and she realized that
the oil lamps were no longer lit. Electric light was doing their job.

And on the wall hung the bridal portrait of Danica
Radulesco—the portrait Dani had last seen in the cottage.

Looking back through the window, she wondered
what that mist had been. Then she closed her eyes, not
wanting to think the thoughts that were coming to her.

But she couldn't shut them out. Just this afternoon, Ion Dobrin had said, "A vampire most commonly enters a room in the form of mist."

Her heart stopped beating for a second. Is that what she'd seen? A vampire coming into the library... coming to harm Karsten?

Frantically, she grabbed the crystal and book of spells and quickly recited the spell that had gotten her to the past.

Nothing happened. Second after interminable second passed before she remembered the spell only worked on the night of a harvest moon.

There was no way of getting back to Karsten for almost a year. She'd never know about the mist, and she couldn't help him if it *was* the vampire. She turned away from the window, feeling a total, utter sense of desolation.

She reached the library door without even realizing she'd been walking toward it. Absently, she paused and picked up an information sheet.

Her eyes skipped over the notes about the desk and the book collection and came to rest on the text about the portrait. Numbly, she read the words:

The large painting is a typical midnineteenth century bridal portrait. The young woman is Danica Radulesco, only daughter of Count Radulesco, whose family owned Castle Ceistra for more than three hundred years.

Sadly, Danica's husband died while fighting in the revolution of 1848–49. After it was over, she left Transylvania and never returned.

There wasn't a word, now, about her coming back and being executed as a vampire. Because, of course, it had never been Danica Radulesco who'd been killed. It had been Dani herself.

But she hadn't been killed. She'd escaped. And the different information sheet reflected that.

So had she somehow changed history? And did that mean Karsten had been right? That his leaving would have changed the history of Transylvania?

Wearily, she shook her head. She didn't know. All she knew was that she'd never see Karsten again. Never hold him or kiss him or make love with him. And she couldn't imagine any worse fate for herself than going through life with nothing but her memories of him.

The lights flicked off and on, warning that there were just ten minutes until closing time.

Dani opened the door and started bleakly down the corridor.

"Dani?"

She stopped midstride, thinking she'd heard Karsten calling her. But, of course, it was only her imagination.

"Dani?" she heard again as she took another step.

She turned, even though she knew she'd see nothing but the open library door.

Instead, she saw an image of Karsten standing in the doorway. She'd thought she was completely cried out, but the image brought fresh tears to her eyes. If she was going to start hallucinating about him, she didn't think she could stand it.

The image smiled at her. One of Karsten's sexiest smiles. "Hey... you don't look glad to see me, Dani. And you'd better be, because I've got no way of getting back until next year's harvest moon."

"Karsten?" she whispered.

The image smiled again.

"Karsten?" She raced back down the hall and straight into his arms.

His oh-so-solid arms.

And then he gave her a kiss that no image could ever even conceive of.

After he'd kissed her thoroughly, he drew back a little and grinned at her.

"What happened?" she demanded, still clinging to him and trying not to laugh out loud with joy. "Oh, Karsten, I'm so, so happy you're here. More than happy. I'm elated and ecstatic and a hundred other words I can't even think of. But I can hardly believe it. What changed your mind?"

"Ion."

"Ion?"

"Uh-huh. Remember his saying that he'd like to see you disappear into the future?"

She nodded.

"Well, he was serious. He'd been standing outside the library window from the time Letcha left, watching. Then, when you disappeared, he came climbing in and—"

"But I saw mist. I saw *mist* coming through the window, Karsten. And I was terrified. I thought it was the vampire coming after you."

"No, the mist was just Ion practicing his magic—thought he'd impress me with a grand entrance. But he...Dani, watching us together made him decide to break his rule about never playing fortune-teller."

"He told you about the future?"

"Some. Enough to let me know I could come after you. He said that I wouldn't turn out to be critical to the movement, after all. There's a freedom fighter in

Bucharest who's going to... but that doesn't matter now. Because everything is going to be resolved just fine without me—and without donating Danica's jewelry to the cause."

Karsten pulled several of the pieces from his pocket and held them out to Dani. "I thought it would be easier for me to adjust to a new world if I had a job. And if you use this to start your company..."

"*Our* company." Dani gave him a huge hug, just to reassure herself that he really was a solid, living man. But when she tilted her head to kiss him he held back, grinning at her again.

"Don't you want to know about the vampire? Ion told me about that, too. Came to his final conclusions this afternoon."

She merely nodded again, not willing to admit that she'd totally forgotten about the vampire riddle.

Karsten waited for an infuriating minute, then said, "Romulus Teodescu."

"What?"

"Well... he isn't *really* a vampire. But he was good enough to fool both of us that day in the cave. And he fooled *everyone* by making his murders look like vampire killings."

"*His* murders? *Romulus* killed all those people?"

"Uh-huh. You were right, Dani. He wanted Castle Ceistra so badly that he was determined to drive my family out. And he figured his best bet was to convince the villagers that there was a vampire on the loose—a Nicholae vampire. That's why he attacked Ernos right in the castle, then left him alive to tell the story."

"But it was Romulus who hired Ion," Dani murmured. "Why would he hire someone to determine who the killer was when it was *him?*"

"Just to show everyone how concerned he was. But Ion turned out to be smarter than our fine mayor expected."

Dani slowly shook her head. Even though Romulus had wanted the villagers to kill her, she could scarcely believe he'd been evil enough to murder all those people. She glanced at Karsten once more, saying, "What will happen to him?"

"He'll be tried. Sentenced. Transylvania in 1850 isn't really as primitive a country as it must have seemed to you, Dani. People just tend to overreact a little when it comes to vampires and witches."

"Transylvania *wasn't,*" she said. "People just *tended.* You'll have to get used to using the past tense," she explained when Karsten looked at her uncertainly. "You're talking about 1850. That's a long, long time ago now."

He exhaled slowly. "This is all going to take me a while to get used to, Dani. There'll be so much I won't understand at first. So much I won't know how to do."

She reached up and wrapped her arms around his neck. "Don't worry," she murmured, threading her fingers through his hair and drawing his lips to hers. "The really important things haven't changed a bit. And you know how to do them perfectly."

MILLION DOLLAR SWEEPSTAKES (III)

No purchase necessary. To enter, follow the directions published. Method of entry may vary. For eligibility, entries must be received no later than March 31, 1996. No liability is assumed for printing errors, lost, late or misdirected entries. Odds of winning are determined by the number of eligible entries distributed and received. Prizewinners will be determined no later than June 30, 1996.

Sweepstakes open to residents of the U.S. (except Puerto Rico), Canada, Europe and Taiwan who are 18 years of age or older. All applicable laws and regulations apply. Sweepstakes offer void wherever prohibited by law. Values of all prizes are in U.S. currency. This sweepstakes is presented by Torstar Corp., its subsidiaries and affiliates, in conjunction with book, merchandise and/or product offerings. For a copy of the Official Rules send a self-addressed, stamped envelope (WA residents need not affix return postage) to: MILLION DOLLAR SWEEPSTAKES (III) Rules, P.O. Box 4573, Blair, NE 68009, USA.

EXTRA BONUS PRIZE DRAWING

No purchase necessary. The Extra Bonus Prize will be awarded in a random drawing to be conducted no later than 5/30/96 from among all entries received. To qualify, entries must be received by 3/31/96 and comply with published directions. Drawing open to residents of the U.S. (except Puerto Rico), Canada, Europe and Taiwan who are 18 years of age or older. All applicable laws and regulations apply; offer void wherever prohibited by law. Odds of winning are dependent upon number of eligibile entries received. Prize is valued in U.S. currency. The offer is presented by Torstar Corp., its subsidiaries and affiliates in conjunction with book, merchandise and/or product offering. For a copy of the Official Rules governing this sweepstakes, send a self-addressed, stamped envelope (WA residents need not affix return postage) to: Extra Bonus Prize Drawing Rules, P.O. Box 4590, Blair, NE 68009, USA.

SWP-H894

This summer, come cruising with Harlequin Books!

PORTS
OF CALL

In July, August and September, excitement, danger and, of course, romance can be found in Lynn Leslie's exciting new miniseries PORTS OF CALL. Not only can you cruise the South Pacific, the Caribbean and the Nile, your journey will also take you to Harlequin Superromance®, Harlequin Intrigue® and Harlequin American Romance®.

- ◆ In July, cruise the South Pacific with SINGAPORE FLING, a Harlequin Superromance
- ◆ NIGHT OF THE NILE from Harlequin Intrigue will heat up your August
- ◆ September is the perfect month for CRUISIN' MR. DIAMOND from Harlequin American Romance

So, cruise through the summer with LYNN LESLIE and HARLEQUIN BOOKS!

CRUISE